QUICKIE

By A.C. Irving

One day my friend Tamica hit me up and told me to check out this girl who wrote stories on Instagram. I checked her out and was so inspired. She wrote stories AND she had created a YouTube series, which is something else I'm working on. If you don't already, go follow @tylertellsstories on Instagram! Moving forward, I took my friends advice and mixed it with my random moments of creativity. And boom, I made my story page! I started my first short story and my readers LOVED it. Now here I am with my short stories in a book! "Quickie" is a book of short stories that I started on Instagram and Twitter! "Quickie" will be a series of short stories. I hope you guys enjoy these juicy quick stories and I look forward to hearing your feedback! P.S. if you guys don't already, please follow my social pages to stay updated.

TABLE OF CONTENTS

ROBYN AND DAMIEN: Robyn stayed down with her man and had the absolute most faith in his change. But because of their history and the damage he had already caused, she was not taking his shit anymore. Heartbreaking news of her now soon to be baby daddy's fresh deceit, changes her whole life.

HANDLE AND SLIM: Slim loved her man but she craved attention from another one. After being caught out there by her lover, she is forced to make some major decisions.

EVE'S BODY: Eve thought a baby could save her relationship until she found out the worst.

CARMEN AND HAZE: Two sex addicts hook up after a meeting and try to figure out ways to spice their sex life up. They figured a kinky sex life would help them to be faithful.

PENELOPE: This little girl told a lie to keep her mom from marrying a man besides her father. Young Penelope had no idea how bad her lie was going to hurt the people she loved.

ROBYN & DAMIEN

The cries of newborn babies eased Robyn's ears as she waited to go home. She loved her job as a neonatal nurse and midwife, but she was newly pregnant, tired, and she missed her man. As she smiled while thinking about her soon to be husband, her phone began to ring. Checking the call, it was her best friend. "Brit, what's up girl? You know I'm at work. I get off in a few," Robyn spoke as she answered the call. "Bitch, I'm looking at Damien right now in Baskin & Robin's and he's in some pregnant bitch's face," Britney got straight to the point. "What!?" Robyn was shocked and didn't believe it. She was sure it was not how her friend was making it seem. "Nah Britney, I don't believe that. Ima call you right back." Robyn hung the phone up and began to FaceTime her man. "If this nigga don't answer this phone, it's gone be a problem," Robyn spoke out loud to herself. On the third ring Damien answered the phone, smiling with his pearly white teeth shining. "Hey baby how's work?" Damien asked, as if nothing was wrong. Robyn felt a little silly that she almost believed her friend. "It's almost over, I miss you, I can't wait to get off." Robyn spoke in her baby voice. "I miss you more babe, I'm getting you and little me some ice cream. I was gone surprise you with it but fuck it you on the phone now," Damien laughed. Robyn smiled as her heart warmed up. She loved how extra caring he was now that she was pregnant. "See that's why we love you," she laughed. "Well let me get back to work. I'll see you in a few babes. Love you," Robyn ended her FaceTime call with Damien and contemplated whether she should call her friend back. She was right about him being in the ice cream store but there was no pregnant girl in sight. She called her back just to make sure everything was everything. "Let me guess...you called him?" Britney said as she answered the phone. Robyn laughed, "bitch you know I did." She responded. "Well call back now cause shawty just came out the bathroom," Britney's words struck Robyn's nerves. "Nah I ain't gone call him. You already know if you calling me to tell me some shit you got to be ready to ride. Now record them bitch and follow him if they're in the same car, and please don't miss a thing...and don't let him see you," Robyn's words upset herself. Here she was going back to the bullshit she thought was over. Britney laughed because she knew her friend was serious. "This nigga ain't do shit in so long I forgot how crazy you could get," Britney spoke. "I'm not playing with this nigga no more Brit. I'm pregnant now, he proposed. This nigga done got dipped in holy water for me. I will kill him if he tries me again," Robyn spoke and meant every word. She loved Damien through his most rough, lowest days and she was never going back to them with him.

"Damn sis, I'm sorry I even called you with this bullshit," Britney said, feeling bad. Maybe she should have just minded her own business, she thought to herself. "Well, it's too late for that now Brit. Follow that nigga and get the footage. Ima hit you back," Robyn ended the call. The rest of her shift was going to be stressful now. She desperately hoped that her friend was mistaken and her soon to be husband was not going back to his old ways. Before a tear could shed, she went to the bathroom to be alone. Taking a deep breath, she didn't know what else to do besides pray. Praying had helped her get through so much. "Dear God, I'm not sure what's going on right now, but I need you to take the wheel. Please calm my mind, body, and soul, and keep me from overreacting. You're my witness that Damien said he'd change Lord, and he has been doing just that. Please don't let it be that he's going back to his old ways. God, I pray that no weapon formed against my relationship, or my family will prosper. I'm afraid of what I'd do if my heart is broken again. It's in your hands lord. Amen." Robyn took a deep breath as she opened her eyes. She pushed all negative thoughts out of her mind and began to believe that her friend had made a mistake. Her man wasn't stupid, and she knew that he did not want to lose her. It's been a long 10 years since she'd been with Damien and the first eight of them were rough. Some would call her a fool for what she put up with but to her, she was just in love.

Damien took a deep breath and looked around. It was normal for Robyn to call him, but he knew he was up to no good. He watched Asia as she wobbled out of the bathroom. Every day he tried to figure out how he was going to get away with having this baby and every day would turn into a new day with no answers. He planned on marrying Robyn, but somehow his heart was with Asia as well. Asia was his high school sweetheart and after she moved away for college, the relationship just didn't work out. They ended on good terms and had no bad blood. She was his first love. She had recently moved back to town and made sure that she got in touch with him. They hit it off like they never separated, and now she was pregnant. The love he had for her ran deep. He was sure the only thing that ruined their relationship was the distance between them. She had no idea about Robyn and now he was stuck between the two. Robyn has had his back through everything. His broke days, his jail phase and especially his hoe ways. He wanted to change so bad for Robyn. He even went to a priest to get prayed over. Now he felt guilty, not only was he cheating, but he had another child on the way. He pushed the thoughts of Robyn out of his head as he paid attention to Asia. He grabbed her hand and they headed out the door to his car. Before opening her car door for her

he kissed her on her forehead.
"You're so beautiful carrying my
son," he told her. Asia blushed. "I'm
so thankful to be giving you one
babe," Asia answered as she kissed
him back on his lips. She climbed
into the car, feeling so loved.
Damien looked around before
getting in his Audi and driving off.
He had to drop her off and make it
home in time to meet Robyn. Britney
sat in shock as she watched her best
friend's soon to be husband treat
this mysterious girl as if she was his

babymama. She recorded everything, right down to the kisses, and she was going to pull off behind him in a few seconds. She wasn't sure if she should have called Robyn right then or waited for Robyn to hit her back like she said. She was sure she had enough evidence, but she did what she was told and followed him.

Britney thought about her friend as she followed Damien. Robyn was so stuck on this man that she wasn't sure if she should have even told her. Even though she sounded serious this time about not accepting his bullshit, she had heard it all before. She didn't want to be the bearer of bad news, but she couldn't un-see what she saw already. She started feeling funny and suddenly wished she had not said anything. Knowing that it was too late now, she continued to follow Damien and the mystery pregnant woman. After about a half hour of driving he finally came to a destination, it was a nice house on what looked like a quiet corner. Britney stayed back as far as she could but close enough to get a good view for Rob. She watched and recorded as Prince charming/Damien got out of the car first and opened the door for his passenger. He was so gentle with her, as if he really cared. He walked her up to the front door and they stood talking for a few minutes. Damien began to rub her belly and it looked as if he was speaking to it. She was sure she couldn't get the audio, but any fool could see what

was going on. After having a convo
with this woman's belly, he kissed it
and then kissed her deeply. It was
almost obvious that this girl was
carrying his child. Britney stopped
recording and sat in disgust. She
knew for sure this would crush her
friend. Damien took his phone out as
he walked back to his car. "I bet his
foul ass is calling Robyn now,"
Britney thought out loud to herself.
She began to pull off before him so
she wouldn't be seen. She wanted to
call Robyn right then, but She just

waited for her call. Her phone began to ring and it cut her thoughts off. "Oh, wow look who finally calls me," she answered her phone as she tried to flirt. "Yo! Why can't you ever mind your business?" Chris sounded annoyed as he questioned Britney. Chris was one of Britney's many niggas. He was her favorite. "What the hell are you talking about Chris? And hi to you too nigga!" she answered confused. She wasn't sure what he was talking about. "Why the fuck are you following that man? Do you get paid to stalk people or something?" Chris asked very upset. Britney felt Stupid. Damien must have spotted her and called him. She felt so stupid and low. Chris continued speaking, and all she could do was listen. "I'm telling you once and only once Brit, mind your fucking business!" Chris tone was so serious. He said what he said and then he hung up. Britney was stuck. She knew Chris meant business, but she had seen too much to not tell her friend. She thought more about it, she was already caught and Damien and Chris would both know who this came from if it got out. She shook her head as she did what she thought was the right thing. *"False alarm girl, I made a mistake,"* she sent Robyn a text feeling guilty. She tried to feel good about it as she thought about Robyn and Damien's relationship. They were engaged. She was pregnant and her friend was happy. Maybe this is the right thing to do. She was confused. Robyn felt relieved after reading the text

Britney sent her. She walked out of work ready to get home and cuddle with her man. She called Britney back while she drove home, but she didn't get an answer. She wanted to call her again but instead she decided to just turn her music up. Robyn pulled up to her luxurious house and was glad to see Damien's car in the driveway. She took a deep breath as she thought about how thankful she was. She had busted her ass working and going to school to finally get her dream job, buy her dream house, and now finally start a family. She knew her man wasn't perfect, but she felt like he was perfect for her and she wouldn't have her life any other way. "Honey I'm home," she called out in a joking manner as she entered her home. "I know babe, I smelled you when you turned the corner. Come here," Damien joked back. He greeted her with a hug and kiss and took her bags from her. "I ran you a bath. Take your clothes off," he told her. Smiling inside and out, Robyn did what she was told. She walked past her man naked and switching, headed for their jacuzzi. Thinking how this was just what she needed, she inhaled deeply as the hot water took over her body. She laid back, closed her eyes, and thought about how good she had it. The hot bath water calmed her nerves, and she remembered her ice cream. "Babe can you bring me my ice cream pleaseee?" She put on her baby voice. "Fuckk," Damien mumbles under his breath. He was so caught up with Asia he forgot Robyn's ice-cream. Walking towards the bathroom he couldn't think of anything else to say besides "Damn babe, do you know it melted and I had to throw it out of my car?" He tried to sound as sincere as possible. "Do you want something else?" he asked her. Robyn tried to hide her attitude. "Nah it's fine, I'll just find another snack when I get out," she put on a fake smile as she spoke. "Okay, my bad about that," Damien apologized before walking away. Robyn tried to stay calm as her mind jumped to a million and one conclusions. She didn't care about the ice cream. She cared more now about him being in the ice cream shop with a female. She didn't believe at all that it had melted, which to her meant he never planned to bring any. He was there with another girl and mentioned ice cream because she called. She wanted to call Britney back but then she thought about her text. She was becoming frustrated and confused.

She made a mental note to call Brit in the morning. She decided not to let her over thinking ruin her mood for the night.

She enjoyed the rest of her bath as she thought about laying down with her man. Even though she knew something was off she was going to believe him for the night. She rubbed her belly as she thought about their unborn child. Damien wanted a boy, but she wanted a girl. She thought about the nursery and the baby shower. She was so excited to become a mom. She had delivered so many babies in hospitals and even in homes, and now it was going to be her turn.

Asia laid in bed as she rubbed her stomach and thought about Damien. She couldn't believe how fast everything was going since she'd been back home. After a bad breakup with her abusive ex Jamel, she was forced to come live with her mother. She planned on staying temporarily and was back and forth until she got things together. But now, she was in too deep with Damien. When reaching back home she didn't expect Damien to be so available, but he was there to mend her broken heart, as if they had never separated. Before she knew it, they were fucking and loving each other like nobody's business. Now, Asia wasn't a fool, she knew that there was no way Damien could be single, but she never asked because she didn't care. She enjoyed her time spent with him and that's all that mattered to her. Damien never brought it up and he wasn't holding back like he had something else going on. So, she simply went with the flow. She was expecting a baby boy in a few months and he seemed more excited than her. She was content with their relationship. "Damien Jr.," she spoke out loud to her stomach as she smiled. "Mommy and daddy loves you king," she said as she rolled over and got comfortable in bed. Her mind went to her ex, Jamel, and her nerves became a little tense. She knew that if anything was going to be a problem, he would. He was deranged, abusive, and a heavy pill popper. She didn't think he would come looking for her but in the back of her head she really never knew. Pushing thoughts of him out of her mind, she grabbed her phone to call Damien to make sure he made it home safely. As always, he picked up by the third ring. "Hey D, you made it home safely?" she asked concerned. "Yes, beautiful I did, I want you to get some rest. I'll call you in the morning. Night babe," Damien hung up the phone quickly. Asia felt some kind of way but didn't trip because at least he answered the phone, she thought. "*I mean, damn just rush me off the phone, but gn honey. I love you,*" she texted him. "*Luv you more,*" he texted back. Asia Smiled as she put her phone down and closed her eyes. She tried to think about the new family she was starting so she could dream about them. She hadn't been this happy since she first started dating Jamel.

She missed this feeling and wouldn't trade it for the world. Damien hung up his phone and took a deep breath. He was slipping and he could feel it. He let Robyn's nosey best friend catch him, forgot the ice cream, and now he was walking out of rooms with Robyn to answer his phone. He knew Rob was going to start tripping soon, but for some reason he didn't care about risking it all. "*You are bugging D, you better get it under control,*" he spoke to himself as he headed back to bed.

He crawled next to Robyn and watched her sleep. He knew she didn't deserve what was going on, but he was going to hide her from it forever if he could.

The first thing on Robyn's mind the next morning was speaking to Britney. She didn't care about the false alarm text, she felt in her heart that something was wrong, and Britney was her only witness. It was her day off, but she still woke up early. Her body was programmed. She watched Damien sleep as she thought about what he could be up to. She wanted so badly to believe that everything was fine and that her man was behaving, but something wasn't sitting right inside her. She felt bad that she didn't believe Britney, but she knew her friend would understand. She just wanted to be sure that everything was a mistake like she had said. Being that it was too early in the morning to bother her friend, she decided to make breakfast. She had not had a day off in a while so why not wake her man up to her special pancakes, she thought. She cooked, cleaned, and showered before waking her man up to breakfast in bed. "Babe wake up its time to eat," she spoke lightly as she tapped Damien's shoulder. "Eat you or eat breakfast?" Damien joked as he smelled his favorite Cinnamon pancakes. He kissed Robyn on her lips and sat up to his plate. The food looked just as good as he knew it would taste. It had been a while since he's had a real home cooked breakfast and he was ready to eat. "Food first, then you can eat me for a snack," Robyn joked back as she smiled. She felt good making Damien feel good. And even though she knew something was wrong, she just wanted everything to be right. She started thinking about whether she should still question Britney. She had no idea what to do. Should she go looking for shit or leave it alone? She was confused. Technically the "shit" came to her first. She started to wish that her friend had never called her with any bad news. As much as she wanted to let it go, she couldn't. Maybe if Damien didn't forget the ice cream her nerves would be more at ease, but they weren't, and it was his fault. Breakfast in bed turned into an hour of love making. Robyn loved every moment of it, and she forgot all about her plans to interrogate her friend. She laid in bed and caught her breath as she smiled at all the nasty things her and Damien had just done together. It turned her on again. Their sex life was amazing, and she had no complaints. She watched Damien get himself dressed for the day after taking a shower. She wanted him to stay in bed all day with her but they both had things to do. She watched her handsome fiancé brush his waves and spray on his cologne. She knew females would want him. He was beyond fine, he was funny, he was a hustler, and he was the most charming thug she had ever known. Robyn rubbed her belly as she thought about her family. No matter what her friend might tell her, she was willing to fight for her man. She drifted off into a nap that she could not resist. Damien watched her sleep as he smiled. He loved Robyn with everything in him, and even though he held one of the grimiest secrets from her, he felt like everything was okay. He had a plan to take care of her nosey friend just in case.

Asia was frustrated as she sat in the waiting room of her doctor's office. She hated coming here and wished she had her own private doctor at home but that was hard to find in this town. She had left several messages with the few midwives she had found, but just about all of them were booked around her due date. Almost seven months pregnant now, she gave up the hope of having a home birth and settled with a black OB she had found through her mother. She wanted a different experience for her first child being born, but she had to take what was available. Finally, they called her name and she rushed to the back, anxious to check on her little man. His heartbeat was healthy, he was positioned well, and he was growing at an above average rate. Asia was relieved that her son was doing great. Now all she wanted was a 3D sonogram so she could see him. Watching the tech glide her tools across her stomach and seeing her baby appear on the screen melted Asia's heart no matter how many times she had seen him. Every appointment filled her up more with love. She was so happy, and she could not wait to hold him. His sonogram revealed his fat face and chunky cheeks. His lips were perfect and poked out as if he was ready for a kiss. Asia smiled at her baby's face. She felt so much joy and love knowing that soon, she would be meeting the love of her life. He looked like Damien in the sonogram, and this made her heart melt more.

She left the office with new pictures to add to her baby photo book and she could not wait to show

Damien the 3D sonogram. She never complained about going to the Dr alone because secretly she wanted that bonding time with her son by herself. She took a deep breath as she thought about Damien. They were about to be parents together and she could not wait to share her life with him. She wondered about the other women in his life. As much time as she got to spend with him, she couldn't see him having a real girlfriend. If anything, maybe a few females he could hit up when he wanted to, but he couldn't have been tied down. Asia knew this was a little too good to be true, but it felt great thinking her baby-daddy was perfect and she had no reason to believe otherwise. She became nervous as she thought about it more. What if she found out something crazy after having the baby and then she is forced to be a single mom? Asia's thoughts went overboard. She stressed herself out thinking about how much her life was about to change. She wanted a two-parent home for her son, and she was going to do whatever she had to do to make it happen. She began to think about how she would bring up the topic to Damien. She needed to let him know that her due date was closer, and things were going to have to change. She wanted to live with him. She was going to mention them moving in together so they could raise the baby the best way possible. They were about to be a family and she saw no sense in them living separately.

Robyn woke up well rested and ready to talk to her friend. She called twice and got no answer, so she sent her a text. Britney always answered back right away unless she was with one of her many men. Robyn decided to give her a minute to respond as she got dressed for the day. She had plans to hang out with her friend today anyway so either way she was going to see her. She put on some music and took her time as she showered. Rubbing her growing tummy made her think about how much her life was about to change. She was finally going to have her own family and she couldn't have been happier. Everything was perfect in her life except this misunderstanding with Britney catching Damien, and she wanted to get to the bottom of it. She was ready for whatever it was, she wanted and needed to know. After her shower she checked her phone to see if Britney had texted her back, but she hadn't. Robyn knew this was unlike her, but just assumed that she was busy getting her freak on. She continued to get dressed and ready to head to her friend's house.

She checked herself out and smiled. She looked good and she felt good. She told herself that even if Britney gave her bad news, it would not change her mood. She was going to be happy no matter what. She shook her head in shame, realizing how much she was doubting her fiancé. It was almost as if she wanted something to be wrong. Confused from her thoughts she hurried up and headed out the door. She was going to put an end to all her wondering. The drive to Britney's house felt longer than usual. Robyn was dreading the possibility of bad news. But she had to ease her mind. Pulling up to Britney's house, Robyn saw her car in the driveway, so she knew she had to be home. She figured she was getting her groove on now and that she would have to interrupt. It wouldn't be the first time Robyn stopped Britney's flow in the state of an emergency like now.

Knocking on the door she waited for an answer. After three minutes of waiting Robyn knocked again. Another three minutes went by, and Britney still had not answered. "I know the penis ain't that good sis," Robyn joked as she laughed out loud. She decided to use her spare key to get in. "B, B it's Rob. I'm using my key and coming in," Robyn yelled out as she let herself into the house. "Britney," she called out again as she closed the door. But there was still no answer.

Robyn heard music playing as she walked towards Britney's room. She assumed that's why she couldn't hear her. She walked into Britney's room and instead of having to hide her eyes from naked bodies she saw her friend laying in the bed looking lifeless. "Britney! "Robyn screamed out as she checked her pulse. It was faint and slow. Robyn began to panic. She immediately called for help. "Hello... 911..". She held her friends head in her lap as she continuously tapped her face trying to wake her up. "Wake up B, wake up please!" Robyn cried out. She could not believe what was going on. "What the fuck did you take girl? What did you do?" Robyn cried. She knew her friend was into many things, but she never imagined that she would try to overdose on anything. Suddenly, thoughts of Damien popped in her head, and she decided to call him. As always, he picked up, "Hey baby you finally up?" He asked answering the phone. Robyn immediately burst into tears.

She felt so guilty worrying about playing detective to her friend while she was home on her death bed. "Baby, I think Britney is dying," Robyn cried out. "I came to her house and she's in the bed unconscious. She looks like she's barely breathing," Robyn cried harder. "Babe, slow down, did you call the police?" Damien asked. "Yes, they're on the way now but she doesn't look good D. I don't know what she did to herself," Robyn continued to cry. "Listen baby calm down, I don't need anything happening to you or my baby. I'm not around right now so I'm going to send someone over there right now. He'll stay with you until I get back from making this move. I'll be there as soon as possible," Damien said trying to calm her down. "Okay babe, just hurry up," Robyn sniffled as the thought of her man coming to her rescue settled her a little. The sounds of sirens began to fill the block and paramedics soon flooded Britney's house. All that Robyn heard was code words being yelled as they took over her best friend's body. They pumped her stomach as they hauled her off into the ambulance. Robyn watched as she cried. "Ma'am are you going to ride with her in the ambulance or meet us at the hospital?" A young woman asked Robyn. "I will meet you guys there," Robyn sniffled as she spoke. She hated ambulances and being pregnant made it worse so she couldn't ride with her friend. "Okay, we're off," the paramedic called out before getting in and closing the doors to the ambulance. Robyn was too distraught to drive but she wanted to beat the ambulance there. She didn't want her friend spending any more time alone. She wasn't sure if she had much time left. Damien's man arrived just in time. Watching the car pull up from the window, Robyn looked around her friend's room before leaving. She decided to pack her a bag for the hospital so she could be comfortable when she woke up.

Robyn's heart hurt thinking of the possibility that she wouldn't wake up. She saw her cell phone on the dresser and decided to bring that for her too. She rushed out of the room, locked up the house and made it outside before Damien's man made it out of his car. Robyn wanted to make it to the hospital right away. She wiped her face and called Damien to let him know he was there. Opening the car door, Robyn realized that she knew Damien's man. "Oh shit, hey Chris" Robyn greeted him with a smile and noticed that he didn't look too good. "What did they say?" He asked, concerned about Britney. Robyn felt sad, "they didn't say...they just rushed her out of here." Robyn spoke. She watched as Chris just shook his head. "I don't know what's going on with her. I can't picture her trying to kill herself, but it seemed like she overdosed on something," Robyn told him. "That ain't like Brit, I don't know what's up but somethings wrong," Chris spoke with an attitude.

Robyn understood that he was scared for her, but she didn't think she deserved his attitude. "She's strong Chris, she's going to pull through," Robyn tried to convince him and herself. "I hope so. I wanna know who did this." Chris looked at Robyn with anger in his eyes. "I want her to tell me who did this to her," Chris spoke, and he meant his words. He was livid inside that someone had harmed her. It made him even more angry that this happened after Damien's threat. He didn't mean to give Robyn attitude, but he was too upset thinking Damien had something to do with this. This would be a major line crossed between them and Chris knew it would not end well at all. Damien was his man's forever, but lately he was letting the money get to his head. Chris didn't know who to trust. He knew that Damien caught Britney following him and was worried about his little secret getting out. Chris looked over at Robyn and her pregnant belly, if only she knew what her fiancé was hiding from her, he thought. He shook his head as he tried to clear his thoughts and focus. He was going to have answers as soon as he got to them. Britney was far from his girl, but he had unconditional love for her. Their relationship was based mostly on sex, but they had built a bond in between them. She was like his home girl with a great vagina. He thought about all the times they had spent together, and he hoped in his heart that she was going to be okay.

Pulling up to the hospital his phone rang, and it was Damien. "How's everything going?" he asked concerned. "I'm not sure yet, I'm just getting here. I'm about to see what's up," Chris responded nonchalantly. "Keep me posted. I'm praying," Damien said as if he cared. "Thanks," Chris answered before hanging up. He put the thoughts of Damien being responsible to the back of his mind as he parked his car and prepared to hear the news from the doctors. He took a deep breath and crossed his fingers. He had faith in Brit. Entering the hospital Chris let Robyn do all the talking. Britney was in ICU, still unconscious and fighting for her life. "It seems like whatever she took or was given is hiding in her system. It's some sort of drug. We're doing everything we can to figure it out," Dr. Jones spoke. Chris and Robyn looked at each other hopelessly. They had no idea what she would have taken. There was nothing they could do but sit and wait to hear from the doctor again. There was an awkward silence as they sat and waited for the update on their friend's life. They both hoped for the best.

Damien smiled as he held the 3D sonogram of his unborn son. He was amazed at how good of a picture it was. He saw so much of himself in his features. Asia wanted him to keep the picture, but he knew that would be impossible with Robyn. He was going to take it and get rid of it. Thinking of Robyn, he knew that he had to hurry up and get home. He knew she was going through it after finding her friend that way. He felt bad for what happened to her, but he knew she was always in someone's business. He didn't trust her not to tell Robyn what she saw. He knew it was just a matter of time before she would spill the beans to Robyn about everything. He did put a warning hit out on her even after telling Chris to talk to her. But near death was never intended. He was not sure if he should be worried that his man went too far or if someone else had done his dirty work for him. Either way he knew Robyn would be in rare form over this.

After hours of praying and waiting, the doctor finally came out and updated Robyn on Britney's condition. She was still in ICU, but she was stable. The medicine they gave her to reverse whatever was in her system was finally breaking through. Whatever drug she took was strong, but it was not strong enough. If she had taken any more though it would have been a fatal outcome. Robyn and Chris took the news in thankfully, worried, and confused. Their friend was going to pull through, but they still had no idea how this happened. The doctor informed Robyn that she could not leave the bag she had packed for Britney in ICU. She could bring it back when Britney was stable and had been moved out of ICU and into her own room. They thanked the doctors and waved to Britney through a glass window. They were more than happy that they could leave the hospital breathing a little easier.

On the drive home it was mostly silent besides the radio playing on low. Britney's phone rang and Robyn remembered she had packed it for her. She was not sure if she should answer it, but she thought she should at least see who was calling in case it was a family member. By the time she retrieved her phone the call was missed, and, on the screen, she saw that it was from someone named Dark. She had no idea who that could be, so she did not think to call it back. Chris watched as she held the cell phone and suggested that she should go through it. "Maybe you can see who the last person was that she was talking to or if she had any plans or something," His voiced sounded so concerned for her. "You're right, that's a good idea," Robyn was excited to play detective. She went straight to her text messages and took her time investigating everything. She was determined to figure out what had happened to her friend or at least come close to something. "Take your time driving. This may take some time," she told Chris as she got comfortable in her seat and began going to work. Most of her messages were regular between people she knew, a lot of them were with her many different niggas, but the one that caught her eye was a message sent to the same number that had called her phone,

Dark. The message read, "Did you work on that situation with Damien? I hope you studied the video".

Robyn knew that there were so many Damien's around, but she also knew in her heart that this was about her Damien. Especially after Britney told her about the girl in the ice cream shop. Robyn thought about the reason she went to her friend's house in the first place. It was to get information in person about what she saw. She would bet money that this message had something to do with that. Video? What video? Robyn thought to herself. Then instantly she went into Britney's photo gallery, she checked the entire album and found nothing. She saw an album entitled, "My Eyes Only," and tried to get in it, but it needed a passcode. "Fuck Brit, what is your damn passcode" she asked out loud as she was getting frustrated. "Password to what? I know all off her passcodes," Chris smiled as he informed Robyn. "Wow really?" Robyn asked as she felt that was very trusting. "Yeah, me and brit was like that. She wasn't my girl or nothing but we, I don't know...we were simply different." Chris spoke sincerely about Britney. He typed in her password and sure enough it was the right one. Anxious, Robyn went through Britney's videos. After passing through so many X-rated videos she finally found the video Britney must have spoken about in the text message. Robyn watched her fiancé hug and kiss on a pregnant woman like he was the luckiest man alive. She watched him be such a gentleman to this woman and kiss on her stomach. Her stomach turned as she replayed the video, and her chest began to pump hard. She could not believe her eyes. As much as she prayed for her relationship, her man was doing the ultimate worse. Not only was he cheating, but it also looked as if he was welcoming a baby very soon. Tears filled up in her eyes and she tried to hold them in. "Take me anywhere but home," Robyn spoke softly to Chris, trying to hide the fact that she was upset. But he had already noticed her eyes. "What happened? What did you find?" Chris asked concerned. "Let's just say my fiancé is a low-down cheating punk pussy ass motherfucker," It wasn't about Britney anymore. Robyn burst into tears. She could not hold it in anymore. She was beyond hurt and being pregnant made her emotions worse. She cried as Chris drove and pulled into a driveway. "I had to stop at my place anyway, you can come inside," Chris spoke. They both got out of the car and Robyn followed him into his man cave. His entire house screamed bachelor pad. There were no feminine touches to his place at all. "Make yourself at home," He spoke to Robyn turning the lights on in his living room. Robyn sat down as she replayed the video over and over. She cried and cried until her eyes ran dry. Chris knew that Damien was foul, but he was going to play oblivious to it all. After doing what he had to do at his house he tried to comfort Robyn. He watched her as she cried and could not help but notice how much prettier she was up-close and personal. She always looked good to him, but he never came this close to really admire her. He pulled her hair out her face and behind her ear and told her to stop crying. "You're way too beautiful for this. And you are about to have a baby, you got to pull yourself together, you cannot let this break you. A dog is always going to be a dog Robyn, but that doesn't mean you can't love him," Chris knew he shouldn't have put in any good words for Damien but really he just didn't want Robyn to feel completely like shit. "If you love him then love him for who he is. Don't try to change him. If you can't handle it anymore let it go. You loved him. You did your part. This is his loss," he tried to cheer her up. Robyn sat quietly just soaking everything in. The video crushed her soul but now she wondered what Britney planned on doing with it.

Why would she lie and say everything was a mistake and clearly this man was committing the ultimate betrayal? Who was this person named Dark in her phone that she was discussing her business with? Robyn had so many unanswered questions that she did not know who to trust. She wished that none of this was going on and that Britney could be here to explain. She did not want to feel like her best friend was betraying her, but it was looking a little fishy.

Her head was spinning, her stomach was turning, and she felt herself about to panic. Robyn changed so much for Damien, and she took so much of his shit, she was tired. She could not explain the feeling that came over her, but it was deeper than hurt. It felt good. It was like pain mixed with pleasure. It felt like Damien's betrayal had awakened something in her that was tired of being asleep. Tears streamed down her face as she smiled. She felt thankful that Damien had cheated again. Now she was going to finally be free. Of course, after getting her payback.

She believed everything Chris told her and she knew she had to get it together. She wiped her face up and decided she would stay with Chris for the night. She looked at him differently after his advice and after feeling like Britney was betraying her. Robyn felt like a fool and like the world was laughing at her. How could Damien act as if he were so happy with their situation and be living a double life? If the pregnant woman was pregnant by him, how the hell did he expect to get away with this? Robyn thought. How could he seem so happy with a woman other than her? Robyn's thoughts were starting to get the best of her, and she did not want to cry again. She had to clear her mind. GIRL FUCK HIM! YOU PRAYED ON THIS SHIT AND NOW GOD IS SHOWING YOU WHAT IT IS! SHOW DAMIEN YOU'RE NO LONGER THE BITCH TO BE PLAYED WITH!

Robyn gave herself the best pep talk. And although she knew it would be way harder to do, she was determined and most of all she was finally ready. She wanted revenge but she wanted peace. She planned on getting just that.

Vulnerable, emotional, horny, and scorned she turned her feelings onto Chris. She did not care about Damien; she did not care about Britney. She was doing whatever she wanted to do. She looked at Chris and before he could say anything, she shoved her tongue in his throat. She let him know she wanted him, and she wanted him right then and there. Robyn spent hours releasing her frustration through orgasm after orgasm on Chris' penis. She fucked him like she had all the right in the world to. Chris did not suggest otherwise. He gave Robyn all the dick she wanted.

After rushing home Damien began to worry when Robyn was not there before him. He waited an hour from the time that he got there before he started calling her phone. Each time he was sent to her voicemail. This was not like Robyn at all, but he knew she was mourning. He still expected her to be home. He doubted she was still with Chris, but he decided to call him anyway since he was the last person Damien knew she was with. The first time he called there was no answer. He called again and this time Chris picked up on the second ring. "Yo, what's up?" Chris answered his phone as he watched Robyn's pregnant breast bounce up and down as she was riding him. "Damn G, it sounds like you busy right now," Damien laughed as he heard Chris breathing deeply. "Sounds like you in some pussy nigga," he laughed again. Chris' dick grew harder inside Robyn. The fact that Damien had no idea that it was Robyn turned him on. "Yeah, I'm getting some juicy pussy right now, this bitch pregnant too. It's extra juicy," Chris laughed hard. He knew that Damien would never guess that he was fucking

Robyn, but he wanted to be funny anyway. He still was not sure if Damien was the one who had tried to kill Britney, so he felt like he was getting revenge just in case. "I know that's right nigga that prego pussy be the best. But I'll let you handle that. I was calling because I was wondering where you left Robyn at, I been calling her," Damien sounded worried. "I brought her home after the hospital, she was real fucked up over Britney. She said you was going to be there soon after," Chris lied through his teeth. "Alright Ima call her again. Good looks," Damien ended the conversation and hung up his phone. He did not like the feel of things at all. He sat up in his rocking chair patiently waiting for Robyn to walk her ass through the door.

Robyn woke up and ran to the bathroom. Her morning sickness remined her that she was pregnant and had to do something fast. After spending the night with Chris, her plan of get back was in full effect. The first thing she had to do was get rid of Damien's baby that was growing inside of her. Robyn thought long and hard before making this decision. Yes, she loved her baby and wanted him or her more than anything in the world, but she wanted a family. She wanted her baby to grow up in love and be loved unconditionally. She despised having to tell her child why they have a sibling outside of their family. She refused to share something so special between her and Damien with anyone else. She had taken too much from him. She wanted better and she knew she deserved it. If she had his baby, she'd be attached to Damien forever, and at this point, she only wanted him dead. So, either way the baby would be fatherless. She was glad that going to an abortion clinic was not necessary. She had delivered babies and had easy access to all medications. After vomiting over the toilet, she showered and dressed to head to work. She thought about how she lied to Damien and told him she stayed at Britney's when really, she stayed at Britney's man's house. She didn't trust a soul, not Britney, not Damien and not Chris. She couldn't tell him what she saw because he was still friends with Damien. She couldn't figure out one good reason why her best friend would hide such evidence of her fiancé cheating from her but show it to a stranger. And what did she plan to do with Damien? Robyn asked herself. Her whole life had changed at the hands of other people. She was determined to take control of how it played out.

"Hey Rosie, today is going to be an early day for me. Samantha is going to cover my shift," Robyn told her supervisor after clocking in. She was only there to get her medication and do a little paperwork. "Your check, not mine," Rosie joked. Robyn sat down at her desk and began pretending to be busy. She wanted to stay for at least an hour so she could call Damien from her job phone. She never brought up what she saw to him, and she wanted him to think everything was perfect between them. She was using the knowledge of his secret to her advantage.

Chris replayed his night with Robyn in his head. Sleeping with her was one of the best times of his life. They had sex all over his house. He never knew hurt; pregnant pussy could be so fulfilling. He never thought about how it would affect Britney because he knew she would never find out. Besides, Britney wasn't his girl anyway. He felt as though she would only have a right to be mad at Robyn. He thought a lot about how it would affect Damien. He wanted him to know so bad that he started filming them fucking after the second round. He never intended on showing him, but he had this little "just in case" feeling deep down inside. He stilled looked at Damien as a suspect in Britney's incident, so he did not feel bad at all. Chris thought it was crazy how Damien's plan had backfired on him and how

Robyn found out his secret anyway. He headed to the hospital to visit Britney. He was tired of calling and being put on hold. He was hoping to hear more good news when he got there, and hopefully she would be awake. He was anxious to hear what happened to her.

"Hey baby, how's your day going?" Robyn asked Damien in her usual baby voice. "It's going good babe. I'm doing some running around. How's work? Did you bring any babies into this world today?" he asked. "No babe not yet," she responded, thinking of how she was going to be taking a baby out of this world today though. She felt a little harsh about her decision, but she knew it was for the best. "Well baby, soon we'll be bringing our own little baby into this world," Damien spoke as if that was all he wanted. This made Robyn hate him even more and feel better about her plan. He knew he was bringing a baby into this world with someone else, yet he still wanted Robyn's. "Yes baby, I

can't wait," Robyn lied. She finished
her conversation before hanging up.
Then she finished up the light work
she had to do on the computer and
headed for the medicine cabinet. She
took pain pills, antibiotics,
mifepristone, and misoprostol. She
grabbed extra of everything to be on
the safe side. She waited for
Samantha to clock in before leaving
for the day. This was one of her
fastest days at work ever. After
leaving, she went on a lunch date by
herself. She sat down and thought

over her plan. Although it was never confirmed to her that Damien had someone else pregnant, Robyn knew from the video that he did. She refused to feel bad about her decisions or try to give herself excuses to be nicer. She knew that she had to make moves fast before her thoughts got the best of her. After lunch, she headed home and began to prepare for a long two days. She popped two pain pills so the medication could be in her system before the miscarriage began. She washed up and got comfortable. She called Damien and told him she'd be leaving work early because she did not feel well. He offered to pick her up and go home with her too, but she insisted that she was okay and just needed to lay down. She told him that she'd be home waiting for him to finish his day's work.

After feeling the pain medication kick in, Robyn swallowed the first set of pills. She laid on her couch and waited for the medication to work. Shortly after swallowing the pills, she felt her uterus cramping and knew it was almost showtime. She would eventually have to go to the hospital to have the fetus removed but she wanted to make sure it was dead. She did not want the hospital assuming she wanted the baby and trying to save it. She was going to take a double dosage of the pills because she was further along than recommended. She absolutely wanted to get rid of Damien's child. She swallowed more pain pills as the cramps began to become more painful. Soon, she was uncomfortable and wished she had decided against this. She had no idea how girls could do this repeatedly. She swallowed more pain pills as the pain became too much for her. She could not walk and could barely move. She rocked back and forth screaming until all the pain medication in her system took over. She began to feel drowsy, high, and eventually numb. She drifted off into sleep and just wanted all of this to be over.

Sharp pains awoke Robyn from her medicated sleep, and she remembered that she was in the middle of a miscarriage. Blood was everywhere and she knew by now that she needed to be at the hospital. She began to act like she was panicking as she called Damien and told him what was going on. She told him that she had already called an ambulance and that he could meet her at the hospital. She hung up with him and then called 911. Before she knew it, she was in the back of an ambulance being rushed to labor and delivery. She thought about how she would react when the doctors tell her that the baby did not make it. She would surely have to cry and seem distraught around Damien.

After reaching the hospital, the doctors moved fast. She was being hooked up to monitors and machines. She heard a lot of codes being called and from the sound of everyone's voices, she knew they

were desperate to save the baby.
Damien arrived just in time as the
doctors came in to introduce
themselves and deliver the bad news.
Dr. Jackson offered his apologies
and told Robyn that her baby did
not make it and that she was
suffering from a miscarriage. He told
her she would have to have a D&C to
remove the remaining tissue from
the fetus. It was a minor surgery.
Robyn watched Damien's eyes
water, and this helped her act. She
began to cry. "No. No doctor

Jackson, please tell me this is a mistake. Why couldn't y'all save my baby?" Robyn cried out, seeming so heartbroken that Doctor Jackson almost cried with her. "I'm so sorry miss. I am so sorry this happened to you." The doctor offered his condolences again before exiting the room. "It's okay baby. This ain't right, but it's gone be okay...I promise." Damien rubbed Robyn's back as he tried to reassure her that everything that she was going through was going to be okay. "No, it's not okay D. It's never going to be okay. We lost our baby. We were supposed to be starting a family." Robyn cried; she was really putting her all into her act. Seeing Damien fall for it made her feel good. He started crying again after watching Robyn cry. "This is my fault, Rob. I should have been made you take off work. I should have been there for you after you found Britney instead of sending Chris. I put too much stress on you and our baby. Damn Roby I am so sorry. I wanted this baby just as bad as you. I promise you we will have a family baby," Damien showed his soft side as he cried to Robyn. She could not help but agree that it was all his fault, but it had nothing to do with the things he named. He wasn't real, he was a fake, those were the reasons for this. She felt so good inside seeing him cry. He was such a snake that she could never be sure now if these tears were sincere, but they were there, and they were heavy. Her heart smiled as she felt her empty stomach. She got rid of his baby and now she was ready for the sweetest part of her revenge.

TWO MONTHS LATER

It had been a long 57 days of pretending to still love Damien, and Robyn was dreading every moment. Even with time she couldn't forgive him. This was her last heartbreak. After the miscarriage, he was trying every way he could to get her pregnant again, but she had secretly gotten on birth control. Today, her pretending was going to end. Britney was well and out of the hospital. She was experimenting with the wrong friends and ended up taking drugs she was allergic to. No one tried to harm her, being curious had gotten her into some bad shit. Robyn never told Britney about Chris of course and neither did he. Britney came clean and told Robyn about the video and even though she already knew, she pretended not to. Britney revealed to Robyn that her friend Dark owed her a favor and was helping. Actually, because of Dark, Robyn was going to have a wonderful revenge.

Robyn received a page on her phone from one of her patients and had to prepare to deliver a baby. Her patient's due date was not for another week, but she knew how pregnancy went. The baby always came on its own time. This patient was a home birth and Robyn had to be prepared to stay for days so she packed a bag. When she got to her patient's home, it was beautiful. It was her first time fully inside and it was so warming. Her patient was in the bed sweating and panting and Robyn could tell that she had been in pain for a while. "I didn't want to call you unless I knew for sure it was time. My contractions are about two minutes apart now and all I think about is pushing," her patient told her through painful breaths. "Well let's bring a baby into this world today," Robyn smiled as she tried to ease her patients' mind. Her patient

was beautiful just like her home.
Robyn knew her baby was going to
fit right in with the beauty. "Did you
call Daddy yet? Does he know
what's going on?" Robyn asked. "No,
I was thinking about waiting until it
was time to really push," her patient
responded. "Well, it's just about
time. You can call him," Robyn told
her patient. She watched her patient
get so excited and spoke to her
partner as if she was deeply in love.
She thought about her own baby.
She did not feel bad at all for what

she did but sometimes she'd catch herself thinking about it. She wondered if it was a girl or boy. She wondered what her baby would have looked like, but she always reassured herself that she would have a real family someday and she would see. Robyn prepared her medications for delivery. This was going to be quick and easy. The first thing she had to do was calm her patient down, she poked a needle through her patient's IV and within seconds her pain was gone. "That was for pain, you should feel much better now," Robyn told her. Her patient smiled and nodded. It was obvious that the meds were kicking in. Robyn poked another needle into her patient's IV that contained the same miscarriage medicine she had given herself and an extra medicine that was going to help speed up the process. "You should be ready to push in no time," Robyn smiled as she spoke to her patient. In fact, within twenty minutes, her patient was ready for delivery.

Her patient started screaming as the cramps began becoming too much. The pain medication was working but she still felt strong, heavy cramps. Robyn talked her patient through delivery and after her last push the baby was born. Robyn tried to keep her cool as she looked at her patient's beautiful baby boy. Even lifeless he was precious. She wrapped the baby in a blanket and laid him down. She knew it was only a matter of time before his mother would want to hold him.

"Why isn't he crying? Why isn't my baby crying? Can I hold him? Let me see him please!" her patient cried out. Robyn turned around and smiled. "He's sleeping love. You should too," Robyn whispered in her patients' ear before poking another syringe in her IV. Within seconds she was fast asleep. Robyn went to the bathroom and removed her disguised wig and oiled off her make up.

"Asia. Asia, I'm here baby. Did we bring a baby into the world today?" Damien screamed out, excited as he rushed into the bedroom. His voice was like bad music to Robyn's ears. "You sure did Damien. But I'm afraid he didn't make it," Robyn held his dead baby's body out to him and pushed him into his arms. "Congratulations," were her last words to him before removing her ring and leaving him in the room with his new baby and new baby's mom.

To Be Continued...

HANDLE & SLIM

Every time I'm with my man, his wife smells me. It's like she just knows when her other half is doing something she doesn't approve of. It's always less than five mins of me getting into his car when she starts calling his phone for senseless things. I'm honestly tired of being quiet just to hear her ask questions like, "How long are you going to be out for?" knowing he's a trapper and he's always in the streets. Or things like, "Your son is about to go to bed."

It's just annoying. I'm okay with my position in his life, but I'm tired. The craziest thing is, we've never slept together, and we've been dating for a year now. I know it sounds crazy but when we first started messing around, he made it clear that he only wanted someone to keep him company. I was fine with that because he was still generous and available. I had my own relationship that was on a bad path and Hassan was my shoulder to cry on. He kept it real with me from the jump and told me he was married. He told me he loved his wife, and he would never physically cheat on her but that he needed something different. He needed someone to listen to him, to understand that under his superman cape he had a side that needed tender love and care. His wife was amazing, but she was a better mother to his children than she was a wife. He always says that he respected her for that and that's why he couldn't sleep with me. He honestly thinks that us living our own lives together isn't considered cheating because we haven't had sex yet. I go with the flow, I have so much fun around him. He takes the stress away when I am with him. He does almost anything I ask him and he's always surprising me with loving gifts. He makes me so happy that my own relationship started doing better. I stopped nagging my man whenever he was out in the streets because now, I had someone to occupy my time. He often gave me cash instead of gifts and I would use it for my man. I was happy and so were both of my men. I thought what I was doing was okay. I never thought about how our relationship with each other would affect his wife or my man, especially since we weren't physically involved. I often asked myself, '*how would I feel if my man had a friend like me? Would I be okay with them doing everything* together that I did with Hassan? As long as they weren't fucking? I know damn well I wouldn't, but I'd often lie to myself and say I would to make my wrong doings feel right. I loved my man to death. We had a rocky ride, but I never wanted to be with anyone else. I wasn't sure about my feelings for Hassan. I mean yes, I enjoyed our time together to the fullest, but did I even like him? Did I ever care about him? Did I have any love for him at all? I sat and questioned myself over and over after my man's words replayed in my head, *"I know about you and your little boyfriend."* That was the last text I got from him, and I've been sitting here sweating bullets ever since. I was stuck, I was confused, and even though I never did anything with this man, I felt foul. I felt like I betrayed myself and my man. As much shit as he did to me, I know I should tell him to take this like I had to take his shit, but I wasn't built like that. The soft spot I had for him was out of this world. I never wanted to disappoint him, I never wanted to disrespect him, and I surely never wanted him to look at me differently. I didn't want him to lose the love he had left for me. I re-read his text over and over and over, trying to figure out how he

knew anything. Hassan and I made sure we were

extra low. We were never in known areas

together, never in the hood together, we were

extra cautious for this very reason. I was at a

loss for words. My shift ended in an hour, then

I'd have to go home and face my man who I

already knew was furious. When I tried to call

him, he banged it on me. I know when he gets

angry and doesn't wanna speak, it means war. I

was so nervous, and I had to figure something

out FAST!

A FEW DAYS EARLIER

"I'm not sure how you want me to tell you this Mr. Hunt, it's not very pleasant, but here it is. This job your wife has been claiming to go to is actually another man. I'm just going to give it to you straight up," said the P.I. who Handle hired to spy on his girl. He took the envelope from him but didn't open it. "What else?" Handle asked. "Everything is in the envelope," the P.I. spoke, he could tell his client didn't want to open it. Handle gave him an okay nod and handed him the rest of the money he owed him. He honestly thought the investigator would've come back with good news that his girl was perfect and was doing exactly what she said she was doing. But he knew in his heart that something wasn't right, or else he wouldn't have hired him. Taking a deep breath, he walked away with the envelope that he knew was going to change his life. Handle sat and thought long and hard before he opened it. He loved Slim with everything in his soul, and he couldn't believe he might have to kill her. Slim was with him from the bottom up, she was the strongest person in his corner after his mother. He thought about all the foul things he had done to her in the past and he almost felt like he deserved this, but he was a nigga. Nigga's cheat, it's just in their nature, he believed. He felt like Slim could've made the choice to leave him, but she decided to stay so she should've remained loyal. He thought about what made him hire the P.I. in the first place. Slim wasn't herself anymore. She wasn't on his back or down his throat like she would usually be. He believed that it was the new job she told him about, but then she started looking extra good. He was never insecure, and he loved that his woman was a bad bitch, but he could tell the difference between when she dressed up for herself and when she dressed up to impress other niggas. He knew his woman for too long and too well to let anything slip past him. She was so happy all the time and she was changing her hair too much. She was spraying extra perfume and wearing sexy underwear every single day. Handle watched her movements for weeks before he thought anything. What saved her at first was the extra money and the extra gifts she was bringing him. He figured she had to be getting the money from somewhere and he assumed it was her "new job" before thinking it was another man. He assumed everything before considering that it

could have been another nigga because he just

knew his bitch. He thought. Her love for him

never changed no matter what he did to her,

and he couldn't understand how now everything

was going downhill. Slim was singing in the

shower more, she was feeling herself more, she

was just too happy for Handle. He loved her

happy, of course, but he missed his bitch being

a bitch. He knew something was off. Opening the

envelope slowly he pulled out one picture before

putting it right back. He couldn't believe his

eyes. There was Slim, sitting in the next nigga's

car smiling ear to ear like she didn't have a care in the world...like she didn't have a real stand-up guy at home. Smiling like everything in her life was so perfect. She sat in his car and smiled as if she was safe. A million thoughts ran through Handle's head, and he knew he had to see the rest of the pictures. *"Is he fucking my bitch? Am I going to see him with his hands on her? Who is this lame ass looking nigga?"* Handle opened the rest of what was in the envelope. There were so many pictures he had to spread them across the table. Sure enough, every new hairstyle that he noticed on Slim was caught in a pic, every outfit that made him pay more attention was worn in these pics. They were at restaurants, movies, lounges, and in the last pic of them all, he saw this unmarked man walking the closest thing to his wife into a hotel and walking out hours later. Handle was a man, but his heart was hurting, and he was confused. He hadn't been doing any type of cheating lately so he couldn't figure out why Slim was stepping out on him. The only thought in Handle's mind was to kill them both. He never tolerated disrespect or disloyalty. Handle felt that even though he cheated on Slim, he was still loyal. The bitches he cheated with meant nothing to him. He would never let a soul disrespect Slim. Anything she caught him in or found out about was the result of her being on her own detective shit. He never meant to hurt her purposely, but he had problems with falling for flesh. Still and all, he would kill for Slim with no questions asked, and here he was looking at her give herself to another man. *"Aight Slim, this is what you want, and this is what you gone get,"* Handle spoke out loud to himself as he carefully placed the pictures back into the envelope. He took his phone out and made a call, "Yo! I need a job done ASAP. Pull up on me when you get time."

As I watched the clock, it seemed like time was moving extra fast. Work never seemed to fly by this quick. I had no idea what I was in store for when getting home, but I knew I had to face it. I wasn't sure if I should call Hassan and put him on or not. *"Put him on,"* I laughed As I re-spoke my words. Put him on to what exactly? There was no way I could allow Hassan to have the upper hand over my man. But damn, what if Handle wanted to hurt him? I was stuck and confused. Hassan was a great friend, but

Handle was my soul. I thought what I was doing was of great benefit to our relationship, and I never thought that this day would come. I started to think more about how Handle could possibly know what was going on. I re-read his text again and I felt the same way I felt the first time I saw it. Maybe he's just playing with me. But I knew better, Handle would never play like this. Taking a deep breath, I looked at the clock again and it was time for me to go. Just that quick, getting into my thoughts made my time go by faster. I packed my desk up and headed home to face my fears. I prayed the entire drive home that this was all a joke, and that Handle knew nothing. As much as I believed in God, I just knew this prayer would not come true. I took my time driving as I thought of a million different stories I could tell. The only problem was, Handle was a smart guy. He was book and street smart, so it was hard to get anything besides the truth past him. My drive home was slow and quiet as I stayed in my thoughts. I Never slept with this man, I never kissed him, I didn't even hold feelings for him. There was no way that I was going to lose my man over him. I'm taking this shit to the grave. As I pulled into our driveway, I swallowed hard and put my game face on. I went into my phone and deleted the text Handle had sent me. I was going to act absolutely normal. Like nothing was wrong. The house was dark and quiet when I opened the door. I shook off all fear because I just knew that Handle had no hard proof and that I was going to change this whole

shit around. "Babe," I called out, but there was no response. Walking into the dining room, our table was lit up with candles and a dinner for two. *'Oh shit,'* I spoke in my head. *'Is this nigga up to something?'* I thought again. "Hey babe, how was work?" Handle's voice startled me as he crept up behind me, massaging my shoulders. Nervous, but staying calm, I moved my head from side to side, embracing his massage. "Mmmm, it was stressful babe, I'm glad to be home," I moaned as his massage felt great. "I'm glad you're home too. I hope you're hungry. I cooked your favorite." Handle was being extra nice, and as much as I needed to keep calm, I was nervous as hell. I can't remember the last time this nigga had dinner made for me after work. "Aww babe, well I'm starving so let's eat," I spoke in a soft voice as

I turned around and gave him a kiss on his lips.
He took my hand and led the way to the table,
pulling my chair out for me to sit. Handle was
acting like a well raised young man on his first
date with a good woman. I wasn't sure how much
longer I could pretend not to be nervous.
Should I eat this food? Should I just tell the
truth? Should I just ask him about his text? My
mind was racing, and I could almost feel the
sweat starting to form on my forehead. Relax
Slim, this nigga ain't gone kill you. Or would
he? My mind was gone. Dinner looked delicious
and safe. I said a silent prayer in my head,

spoke my grace, and began to eat. "So did you get my text?" Handle was very straight-forward. Almost choking on my food, I kept it calm, "no babe, what text?" I replied lying but trying to sound truthful. Handle looked me right in the eyes as he spoke, "Some niggas was chattin' in the barbershop. They said you've been riding around with some guy in a black Benz. Is that true?" He kept his eyes on me until I responded. The first thing I thought was that he had no proof, but how the hell did he know Hassan had a black Benz? I was almost ready to tell the truth, but I knew it would sound crazy and he wouldn't believe me. "Well damn them niggas must be by my job. I got a ride from a friend from work the other day to get lunch. Delivery was down so we had to pick it up," I answered fast and sounded so stupid. Why the fuck would I tell him I went to get lunch with a guy? It was too late now, what was said was said. "Oh, so niggas are takin' you out on dates for your lunch break now?" Handle laughed and I wasn't sure if he was joking or serious. I rolled my eyes as if he was crazy. "Nigga please," I let out a little laugh before I continued. "Now you know damn well ain't no nigga taking me on no dates. I'm telling you; delivery was down that day and they were short-staffed, so we had to pick it up. It wasn't just me and him either, Sabrina came with us," I lied more. I figured if I put a girl into the equation, it wouldn't seem so bad. I watched Handle's facial expressions and for some reason, I couldn't figure them out like I normally would be able to. I couldn't read him at all. "Oh, Sabrina went too. Ok ok," Handle spoke both sarcastically and like he believed me. I didn't know what to think now but I tried to switch it around. "I know you ain't about to believe no random niggas in no barbershop," I tried to sound offended. "You should know ya bitch better than that. Don't play with me," I tried to sound as convincing as possible. I tried to make him feel bad for even asking me. I wasn't sure if it was working but I was trying. "You're absolutely right. I know my bitch better than that," Handle spoke as he got up from the table. "I know you've been working hard with the new second job and all, putting in all these hours. So, I just wanted to show you some appreciation tonight." Handle changed the whole mood and threw me off guard. He must believe me, I thought to myself. "Aww babe, this is why I love you."

I finished my food and followed him into our master bedroom. He had a bubble bath running for me and more candles lit. *Oh he must want some super head tonight,* I thought as I smiled. *Maybe the rumor he heard made him realize he needs to stop playing with me.* I laughed to myself. With no hesitation, I took my clothes off and stepped slowly into the steaming hot bath. It felt so soothing to my skin. By the time I sat down, I was relaxed. After about 6 minutes, I called out for my man to join me. "H where you at babe. Come get in here with me," I whined with my baby voice on. No response. "Babbbyyy," I called out again. My bath was feeling too good to be in alone. Assuming he couldn't hear me from the bathroom I started to get out of the tub to go get him myself. Suddenly the door opened, and Handle walked in with a blank look on his face. A second later he had a gun pointed directly to my forehead, exactly between my eyes. "Who the fuck is the nigga in the black Benz?" Before I could breathe, blink, or respond, he cocked it back. "And I dare you to lie," Handle spoke with no life in his voice. He stared with no life in his eyes. I had never in my life seen him like this, and my mother fucking heart stopped beating.

Handle held his gun point blank in Slim's face and his finger was on the trigger sweating. He watched how fear crept over her entire existence and he wished she had never played with him. He never thought he would have to kill her, but he always knew any female he gave his heart, could only leave his life through death, quicker if she crossed him. No matter what he did, he expected more from Slim. He expected her to always be herself. "You lied to my face at dinner, and I want you to try it again. Who the fuck is the nigga in the black Benz?" Handle asked for the last time, and he wasn't going to ask again. He watched as tears formed in his girl's eyes and this time it had no effect on him. "Handle, I swear to God on everything we have I'm not fucking him. I be going places with this nigga. He spends money, it's just good company. I'm so sorry. I would never cross you. I know this sounds crazy, but I was just using this nigga. The most we ever did was hug. It's like he pays me for my time and my listening ears. It's like a sugar daddy with no sugar. H you know me," Slim's words felt good to Handles ears, but he didn't trust Her anymore. "Don't fucking call me H. Don't you fucking call me that." Handle's switch flipped and his sense was gone. He pressed his gun into Slims forehead, and she closed her eyes as she continued to plead her truth. "Yo! I'm sorry Handle. I started talking to this nigga when we were beefing. That's all it was, just conversation! I swear!" Slim cried out loud. "Slim, don't you know you're in my blood and soul? Everything about you floats through my body. I was the only person I allowed to hurt you because I knew it was never on purpose and I could always fix it. I would kill for you, be killed for you, and kill you if I had to. Don't you know there's no deeper connection than that?" Handle's feelings were slipping out, but he didn't care. "You think I would let another nigga have you after a part of me is with you? Why would you think that? I don't believe a word coming off your tongue. You went to telly's with this nigga and you want me to believe y'all motherfuckers was just hugging? Slim, I don't give a fuck how many hoes I fucked, that meant nothing to me, you my rib bitch you're supposed to stay solid. How a nigga gets you to fold on me?" Handle moved the gun out of Slims face and placed his hands on his head. He was livid, he was hurt, and he was confused. He wanted to believe her, but he couldn't. "Handle I'll call this nigga right now and prove it to you," Slim spoke through her cries. "Bitch, you probably got that nigga trained to lie. You can't prove shit. You wanna prove something set that nigga up," Handle was just saying anything until he thought about it. 'Yeah, she's gonna set this so-called sugar daddy ass nigga up' he thought to himself. "Matter fact bitch, call him right now. Ain't it almost time for your "night shift?" Get that nigga on the phone and set something up for TONIGHT!" Handle meant business and he was ready.

My legs shook as I tried to get out of the tub. My wrists were weak, and I couldn't hold my weight. My nerves were disturbed as I kept seeing the barrel of Handle's gun in my face. Everything was happening too fast, and I had never been more terrified. I had no choice but to call Hassan. I rushed to my phone. My life depended on it. Taking a deep breath, I tried to get my mind together so I could make this phone call. No questions asked, I was going to set Hassan up. I didn't have time to think and figure a damn thing out about my feelings for him. At this point, I didn't have any. H was my man and after he pulled his gun out, I knew he wasn't playing around about me. Shit got real and shit got deep, and it was only going to get deeper. Seeing Handle watch my every move made me even more nervous than I was. I needed to relax, but it was too hard. "Handle, I'm all the way with whatever you say but can you just tell me that you aren't going to kill me? My nerves are dancing, and I need to calm down. Just please, put the gun away or something," I cried to him looking into his eyes. "Slim, I don't wanna kill you. Just don't make me," he answered with no emotion. He put the gun in his back pocket and backed a few steps away from me. Feeling a little more comfortable, I threw some clothes on and got ready to put on an act. I was planning on seeing Hassan tonight anyway, but now I had to change things around. I had absolutely no idea how this was going to go or what the hell I was trying to do. I knew first things first...I had to prove to Handle that I wasn't fucking Hassan. I closed my eyes and took one last deep breath as the phone rang. "Put it on speaker," Handle's voice reminded me I had to do this the right way. "Naomi, hello how are you?" Hassan's voice came through my speaker and this time it made my skin crawl. Usually, I'd be excited, but with my man knowing and listening, his voice gave me an attitude. I had to get it together if I was going to get this to work. Closing my eyes, I put on my fake English accent and spoke to my side nigga as if Handle wasn't there. "I'm great, I can't wait to see you. I need to tell you something," I replied. "I missed you all day. Is everything alright? What's wrong?" Hassan was

concerned. "Yes honey, everything is fine. I've

just been thinking lately," I lied to him.

"Thinking about what Naa? Talk to me. You know

you can tell me anything," Hassan's voice was

becoming annoying the more he spoke to me.

"Well, I think I want to take this to the next

level. I know what we agreed on but I'm feeling

different lately," I lied more, trying to prove to

my man that I've never been physical with

Hassan. I prayed this would work. "What exactly

do you mean next level? I mean you know both

of our situations Naomi," Hassan replied.

"Hassan, I'm ready to have sex. That's what I mean by next level. I know we could never have a relationship." I was hoping and wishing that this was convincing enough for Handle. I was hoping and wishing. "Oh, wow Naomi I've been waiting for you to be ready. When I made the rules in the beginning, I thought I would be able to stick to them, but it's becoming too hard to resist. Your vibe is amazing, and I could just imagine how good your insides would be." Hassan's words saved my life. "Wow Hassan, so you don't care about your wife anymore?"

I tried to continue playing it off even though he's said enough. "I will always care about my wife. I've been respecting this no sex thing with us because of her but I care about your needs as well." Hassan was still a dog even though he made it sound good. "Well, I guess tonight's our big night. Are we doing dinner before the hotel?" I asked. "Actually honey, some business came up and I have to make a run. I was going to call you afterwards." Hassan was changing plans, but this could be good I thought. "Wow, now I have to wait longer to see you? How long is your run going to take babe? I miss you and I'm horny," I threw my innocent voice on heavy hoping he'd invite me for the ride. If he was making a run that means he'd have a lot of cash on him, and this could be perfect for Handle. "I would tell you to come but I know you don't like people seeing you," Hassan giggled but he was damn sure right. "Well, I don't mind. We're about to take things to the next level anyway," I joked back and giggled with him. "I hope you look extra pretty tonight," Hassan spoke. "I sure will. So should I meet you same-place-same-time?" I asked. "Well, if you want to come on the run, you can meet me at the same place, but can you be ready in an hour?" Hassan asked. "Now I need a little more time than that babe you know me," I joked with Hassan. "Okay you have an hour and ten minutes," he joked back with me. "Well let me hurry then, see you soon," I spoke as I hung the phone up. I was scared to turn and look at Handle, but I had to. He was starring right at me as if he had his eyes on me the whole time. "I wanna pistol whip you so bad but I know you gotta go see this nigga. You out here living a double fucking life. Who the fuck is Naomi? How the fuck you speaking with that dumb ass accent? I don't even know who you are right now. The only reason you're breathing is because you ain't fuck!" Handle was still livid, but I didn't see murder in his eyes anymore. "Honestly, I can explain all of that. I don't know, I just didn't want him to know who I really was." I wasn't sure if it made any sense to him, but I was being honest. "Well, is your name even Slim?" Handle was serious but he also sounded like he wanted to joke about it. I smiled trying to loosen things up. "Slim is my name. You get the real me H," I tried too hard to convince him and secure his trust. I looked him right in his eyes as I spoke. I knew he wouldn't fall for it right away, but I knew he wasn't all the way gone. I still had him, even under all his disappointment and anger. "Now I've never been on a run with him before, but he tells me all about them. I've been with him to enough traps to know that his people spend big money. So, this might be good."

I tried to change the mood and remind Handle that this nigga didn't matter. He was about to be a come up and I was going to cut him completely off. It was awkward speaking about another man to him but at least we were speaking about money. Handle and I were both always about a dollar. "There's a secret spot I always meet him at and I usually leave my car parked there and ride with him. You can follow us," I tried to give Handle the plan. "You mean the tunnel in the park? Yeah, it ain't so secret anymore. I'm not following shit. I'm getting in the car with you. You need to find out when he's going to have the money with him for this run y'all think y'all going on," Handle spoke, making it clear that he was in charge. I had no idea how the hell he knew about the tunnel in the park but it's obvious he was doing his homework. But damn, who was he getting his information from. "Aight H, whatever you say, however you wanna do it. I'm going to get ready so I can be on time. I hope you know that no matter what I love you and only you." I was positive he didn't wanna hear that, but I wanted to tell him anyway.

Walking away, I went into my closet and picked out my sexiest dress. I tried not to think about Handle as I got ready. I was going to make sure I looked extra good tonight because I needed all of Hassan's attention. I had no idea how this was going but I had to have him open.

Handle sat on the bed and his mind was blown. Listening to Slim be another bitch for another nigga fucked his head up. He started to regret some of the shit he did to her, and he started to over think. He was breathing easier since he heard the nigga admit he ain't hit it. But he still didn't like the situation. He almost felt like it was worse that they weren't fucking because they were building a bond. He despised the way they laughed and joked on the phone. He started to wonder if Slim was really pretending or if she loved him. Either way, he was going to find out tonight. He sat on the pictures the PI gave him for two days and he knew how he was going to end it. It was premeditation at its finest. He planned on catching two bodies but Slim might've saved herself. His phone rings and he answer, "Yo! You're actually calling at the right time. Did you do that from earlier?" Handle's thought switched to business. "Aight my nigga that's what I'm talking about. Yo! Some new shit popped up. Some h2 type shit. I need you to round up for the party." Handle always spoke in code over the phone. "Tonight, be ready in 30 type shit." Handle spoke as he hung up the phone. He felt good.

The night wasn't going as he planned, but it was working more in his favor. He looked into the room at Slim and watched her get dressed. He started to get angry all over again. She was beautiful indeed, but now she was a snake to him. But he couldn't deny that he'd still keep her as a pet. He still loved her, but he was disappointed, and he was embarrassed. She had murder on his mind, and she didn't even give her goods up. He hated that his feelings were uncontrollable right now. They were hurting and they were showing. He laughed a little because his mom always told him that he wasn't going to be able to handle it when Slim was ready to be like him. He would always tell her Slim was better than that and that she never would. "Never say never," he spoke out loud to himself as he laughed again. Slim was stepping out on him, and he couldn't handle it. "Momma was right," he giggled again as he calmed down a little. Walking into the room, Slim was fully dressed, and she looked amazing. He wanted to fuck her and strangle her at the same time. "You look nice bitch," He gave her a compliment, but he didn't want to. She was looking too good to go be in the next nigga's face. But at the same time, he was getting money out of it.

Handle started to think about all the shit she was giving him that must've been coming from her nigga. Sometimes she'd surprise him with a few hundred-dollar bills in a card, $1000 gifts, paying bills when it wasn't her turn, all good shit. He started to think how he reaped the benefits of her cheating. He didn't care if she fucked him or not, she still cheated in his eyes. But at least she was getting something out of her wrongdoing. All Handle ever got was caught up and headaches. He had to admit, Slim played him really well. She was good at everything she did, and that was one of the reasons why he loved her. Although, he never thought she'd be good at breaking his man-heart. Handle considered his man-heart as the only heart a man is supposed to have. And really, the only heart that a man is supposed to have, is for his mother, his siblings if he had any, and his wife and his children. Family could be included, but sometimes family wasn't family to him. Everything else gets shown no love. He grew up witnessing how love would get you killed. Slim hurt his man-heart. He brushed it off as he got mentally prepared for tonight's events. He was going to ride in the back seat of Slims car while she drove to meet her nigga. There was no way he was letting her ride alone and be able to give this man a heads up about anything. He still didn't trust Slim; he wasn't sure who's side she was really on. His heart knew that she was with him, but his mind was more on point. He didn't know who she was right now, she was scared, and she was under pressure. He felt that she was doing anything he told her to do, not because she wanted to, but so that she wouldn't lose her life. At least if she decided to switch when she got with him, he would be right behind the car ready to light it up. Handle's thoughts were deep.

I looked myself up and down in the mirror for the last time and Handle was right, I looked great. I wanted to melt Hassan's heart tonight and gain his full attention for whatever Handle had planned. My nerves were so much better, but I knew I wasn't in the clear yet. Handle was right over my shoulder watching me. I don't know what he was thinking but he was definitely in another world. I could tell by his eyes. He didn't want to kill me anymore though; I could tell that too. When he was holding the gun to my face his eyes were unexplainable...eyes I've never seen before. I was just glad he was calm now. I checked my make-up for the last time, and I was ready to go. I walked in front of Handle and looked him in his eyes. "Why you watching me?" I tried to flirt with him to loosen him up a little more. I would always ask him this and he would usually respond with something sweet or something freaky. I waited for a response, but he didn't speak. He just looked me in my eyes. "Why you watching me?" I asked him again with a little more base in my tone to let him know he better flirt back. He was quiet for a few seconds before responding. "Because I wanna hurt you," he spoke like he meant his words. "I'm honestly sorry. Don't hurt me. I hurt myself enough by hurting you. I feel like shit and my soul is hurting. I know you don't trust me but you gotta know that this right here is the real me. This is your Slim fit. That other shit ain't me, it's an act." I was trying so hard to get through to Handle.

I placed my hand on his face as I continued to speak to him. "All the shit we've been through you know me inside and out. You know I'm filled with you. I'm better than your homeboys. I'm a reflection of you. This shit doesn't mean a thing." I waited for him to speak but he still wasn't talking. I took my hand off his face and touched his penis through his sweatpants. He moved a little but not enough to move my hand off him, so I rubbed more. I wanted him to come back from whatever dark place he was in. I needed him to know I was still on his side. He allowed me to rub more on his dick so that was a good sign. As soon as I thought I was getting somewhere with Handle my phone rang and it was Hassan. Handle automatically got an attitude and moved away from me. "Your nigga calling," he laughed sarcastically as he walked. "Shut the fuck up," I yelled to him before answering the phone with my fake accent. "Hey babe, are you ready for me?" I flirted with Hassan. "Yes, you can start heading that way now. I can't wait to see you," Hassan flirted back. "Okay, I'll see you soon. I'm getting ready to leave now." I hung up and turned to Handle. "That's not my nigga, stop playing with me. Let's go it's time to hit a lick." I gained extra courage as I spoke like 'Handle.' He had me shook but I had to let him know I was still Slim. I grabbed my new trench coat and was ready to get this over with. Handle followed behind me as I left the bedroom and walked to the door. I looked around our home that held so many memories. Good and bad, a lot went on between us behind these walls. We were on our way out to make more memories in the world. Handle walked out after me and I locked the house up. I got in my car, he got in the back seat. The ride was going to be a while, the park we were meeting at was a few towns over. I wanted Handle to talk to me. I wanted shit to be normal, but I realized more and more that I had fucked up. I had changed him and now, and he no longer knew how to be with me. I accepted it but I wasn't giving up on trying to change it. I started the car and headed to our destination. I tried to imagine what was about to happen. I wondered if Handle was only going to rob Hassan. Was he going to rough us both up and make it look like a robbery? I tried to think of what the hell I was going to do myself. How do I find out if he had the money with him or not? I don't get personal when we talk about him trapping so I couldn't ask him any questions. "So how is this going Handle?

What's the plan? You can at least speak to me and tell me that," I broke the silence and tried to get him to talk. "I'm going to follow behind y'all in your car. You need to find out if he has the money on him or not. I'll handle everything else." Handle spoke but I could tell he didn't want to. "Okay so how do I let you know if he does?" I asked him. "I'll be calling you, so make sure you answer. One iffy move and it's over for both of y'all." He meant his words. I tried to stay calm and not get nervous. "Aight," was all I could say. I started wondering if Hassan was going to live through this. I

183

wondered if Handle was going to kill him. I started to feel a little guilty. Maybe I should've never started talking to Hassan. But damn that's all it was, talking. I started to think about whether I had any feelings for him. I started thinking about all the fun stuff we've done together. Damn, Hassan was like a best friend to me. We could talk for hours while doing nothing and have so much fun doing everything. I was confused. Handle was my world, I loved him more than he loved Himself. I was confused again. I looked at Handle, he was already planning to kill me again right along with

Hassan. Was this nigga going to hold a grudge against me forever even after I cut Hassan off? Was it going to be the same? Shit, Handle might want to kill me in a week for all I know. I thought about what would happen if I put Hassan on to Handle. I wondered if Hassan would save me. I wondered if Hassan loved me...and loved me enough to possibly have to hurt Handle. Damn, I couldn't believe I was thinking about turning on Handle. I loved him but I didn't know who he was right now, and I didn't know if he was going to stay this way or come back to normal. I saw his eyes change back but now his attitude was speaking differently. I loved him but I wasn't sure if I should trust him. I couldn't believe I was having mixed emotions. I shook all these thoughts out of my head and focused on the road. I was a few seconds away from the tunnel in the park and everything was going to change once I got with Hassan.

I prepared myself to get back into my act and do what I had to do. "So, this is it Handle, it's showtime! I'm ready for whatever you're ready for," I told him as I parked the car. "Well, I'm ready to die," was all he said. "I'll die with you any day," I told him as I got out of the car. I walked slowly to Hassan's car as I thought about Handle's response. I'm not ready to die and Handle only had murder on his mind. I was not going to let Handle kill me. I honestly didn't want him to kill Hassan either. I planned for him to rob him and that's all. I was going to cut Hassan off and move on with my life. But if I decided to stay with Hassan, I wondered if he would leave his wife. I understood the rules he set in the beginning but that was before we clicked. I know he must feel differently about certain things now. I was stuck. I opened the passenger door of Hassan's car with a huge smile on my face putting my fake accent back on. "Hey you, I missed you," I told him. "I missed you more. You smell awesome," he said as I closed the door and sat comfortably. "Well thank you," I flirted and laughed a little bit. "So, what's on our agenda for the night?" I asked him, eager to hear it. "Well, I figured we could grab some take out from somewhere and eat on the way." His voice was so relaxing. He made me feel so comfortable. "Okay a road trip sounds cool," I answered like I was excited to be with him. "What are we going to eat?" I asked. "Um, I was thinking some Jamaican food. What you think?" He asked me. "That's cool," I responded. There was an awkward silence as he drove while I stared out the window. I was completely stuck on what I should do. Suddenly my phone vibrated, and it was a text from Handle. "What's going on?" I texted him back. "I don't know anything yet we're stopping at the Jamaican spot for food." Handle texts back, "Lol how cute." I shook my head and didn't respond. I was tired of Handle's smart remarks. I mean I get it, but it was annoying now. It made me feel more like he was always going to be an asshole now. I thought

about telling Hassan again, but the thought left
as quick as it came. I was going to just relax
and go with the flow.

Hassan's phone rang and broke the
silence. I assumed it was his wife, but he didn't
ask me to be quiet. "I was just about to grab
some food, what's the word?" he spoke, and I
listened. "Man come on now this was not a part
of the plan. I really don't have the time. This
is cutting into my night," Hassan sounded upset
over the phone call. "How long is it going to be?
I can't just be around with all this shit on me
bro. Come on now!" Hassan was more upset, and

I figured the 'shit' he was referring to was either drugs or money. "Man aight!" Hassan hung his phone up with an attitude. "Everything alright babe?" I asked him, sounding concerned. "Business just going wrong that's all. So, let's talk about what you said on the phone earlier," he switched the topic. "I mean, I'm ready," I lied. "Well good because the run we were going to take is pushed back now. So how about we grab this food and get a room 'til it's time to go?" He smiled as he spoke. I started to worry if this was good or not, but I tried not to show it on my face. I smiled back as I spoke, "perfect." I lied again. I had no idea how this was going to turn out. I took my phone out and texted Handle to let him know what was going on. *"His run is pushed back so we're going to the motel. I know he has something on him so check the car."* Maybe this was good. If Handle robbed his car, he wouldn't have to physically harm Hassan. We'd come out of the motel room both confused, seeing the car wrecked. But damn, did I have to really fuck Hassan now? I led him to believe that's what I wanted, and now our time was coming. My mind was all over the place, and I just wished this was all a bad dream. But it wasn't, it was my reality, and I had no choice but to deal with it. Handle texted me back "Yeah aight Slim. See you soon." I had no idea what his message meant but it didn't seem good. I was over this shit. I was starting to get angry. As many times as I had caught Handle cheating, I could never take shit this far. I would have but he never let me, I was always supposed to be strong and handle the shit. Now here he was, mad over me just having a friend and everyone's life was in danger. This wasn't fair and I wasn't liking it anymore. I still had no idea what I could possibly do. I didn't respond back. "I can't wait to get to the room, I'm excited," I lied as I tried to change my mood. I wasn't excited at all. I had no idea what Handle had planned. For all I knew he could kill both of us. I had to figure out what I was going to do, and I had to figure it out fast. "I don't think you're as excited as I am babe," he replied. "Do you wanna skip the Jamaican spot and just order in at the room?" He asked me as he winked. I had no appetite, so I didn't care. My mind was hard to keep focused. "Sure! That's fine," I replied. Now I had to text Handle again. "Change of plans we're going straight to the room *I'll let you know the room number.*" I didn't wanna text Handle anymore and I didn't want to read his response. I was tired of all this shit...the whole damn thing. I didn't want to go through with it anymore, but I knew I really had no choice at this point. We pulled up to the motel and Hassan parked. He got out and opened my door for me like he always did. He was such a gentleman. "Thank you," I smiled. "No, thank you honey," he replied as he watched me get out of his car looking me up and down. "You are a beautiful creation," he told me, and I blushed for real. I knew I looked good, but I would always get mushy over compliments. "Aww thank you Hassan. You're such a great person inside and out I hope you know that." I wasn't sure where my words came from but that's what my mind wanted to say at the time. He looked at me a little shocked but like he appreciated what I said. "You're an amazing person Naomi, I've never met someone like you before and I just want you to know that. No matter what happens between us I wish the best for you," I could tell he meant his words. "I love you," I told him out of nowhere and I completely shocked myself. What the hell was I talking about and what was I thinking? I really surprised myself. He looked at me and was quiet for a moment. "Do you mean that?" He asked me while keeping his eyes on me. I wasn't sure but I couldn't believe I said it. "Yes, I do mean it Hassan. I love you and this time spent with you has been amazing," I was really into my role, but it felt real. I wasn't sure where my words were coming from, but I felt like I meant them. Hassan was quiet and I started to feel like I made him nervous. He just smiled, grabbed my hand, and led the way into the building. He checked us in, and we headed to the elevator. We were still in silence, and I wondered what he was thinking. Did I say too much, or did I say just enough? I wasn't sure. We got off on the 5th floor. My mind started to race again as we got closer to our room. I was so unsure of what was about to happen. If Handle didn't come into the room, would I have to sleep with Hassan? And if he came into the room, was he going to kill Hassan? What did I want to do? I had no idea.

Handle was tired of driving behind Slim and her nigga trying to assume what they were talking about. He wanted to shoot the car up badly, but he knew he couldn't. He had other plans and he was anxious. He watched this random man lead his woman into the building and he couldn't wait to follow them. He looked around to make sure there were no cameras in the parking lot. He broke into the car and popped the trunk. It was empty. Before getting upset he checked the trunk completely. He found a secret compartment and under it was a ton of money. Handle stepped back at first. He looked around again to make sure no one was looking. This was way more money than he expected. He must've been buying a large number of drugs, Handle thought as he was proud of his findings. He went back to his car and grabbed a bag. He stuffed every single stack into his bag as fast as he could. Handle had money of his own, but this was a great come up for him, especially considering who the nigga was. He thought about taking the money and saying fuck both of them, but his pride was in the way. He felt disrespected and he wasn't letting it slide. After packing the money up, he made a call and had one of his boys come move Hassan's car. Handle had all types of friends that could do all types of things. There was almost nothing he couldn't get done. After being sure his car was out of the way he sent Slim a text, "what room number?" He wasn't done, the money wasn't enough. "502," she answered. He read the room number and called his friend who had been waiting on him. "It's showtime. We in room 502, let's get it," he ended his call and was ready for action. The money he found put him in a great mood. He couldn't wait to spend his bitch's dead man's money. He thought about Slim and how her sneakiness got them where they were. He couldn't deny the fact that Slim made all this possible. It was about to get ugly, and Handle felt it was all her fault.

I sat on the bed nervous as hell after I texted Handle the room number. I just knew he was going to come busting through the door any second. I had no idea what he was going to do but I couldn't sit here and pretend with Hassan anymore. I thought I had this under control. I thought I knew what I was doing, but I didn't. This shit was way above me now. I was not ready to lose my life or be responsible for Hassan losing his. My thoughts were interrupted as someone knocked on our room door. My heart dropped but I stayed cool. I looked at Hassan confused as he looked at me. "Who is it?" he asked. "Room service," a lady's voice spoke. I breathed a little easier. "Come in," Hassan spoke, and the door opened. In walked one of the most beautiful women I'd ever seen. She had my full attention, and I couldn't believe she was working as room service. Then, I realized she wasn't wearing a uniform, and she and Hassan locked eyes. Hassan immediately looked like he had seen a pack of wolves coming at him or something. His face was so scared that I was scared for him. "Oh! This is your business trip"

The woman asked him. "Honey, I swear I could explain," Hassan started to speak but she cut him off. "Shut the fuck up Hassan. You can't explain shit. Do you know what the fuck I just went through? I was kidnapped and tortured all day because of your lying, snake, bitch ass," the woman was hurt. I instantly put it together that this was his wife. His fucking wife. "What do you mean kidnapped? What the fuck do you mean tortured honey? What the hell happened to you?" Hassan was so concerned it was sickening. He was just ready to love all over me and now he was crying for his wife. The next thing I knew, Handle walked into the room. Now I was nervous, and I knew some shit was about to go down. Handle had a gun in his hand and death in his eyes. I stood up and was ready for everything to get crazy. "I had her kidnapped and touched on since you thought it was cool to touch on my bitch," Handle was face to face with Hassan speaking to him. "So that's what this is about?" The wife asked before Hassan could say anything to Handle. "Oh yeah! That's right, you don't know your husband here has been sneaking around with my wife for some time now," Handle laughed as everything was unfolding. "So, I decided to join in on the party," Handle spoke to the wife with a big smile on his face as if he was amused. "Go ahead Hassan, tell your wife the truth," Handle spoke directly to him. "Honey, I just met this bitch tonight. She's a trick. I don't know what this crazy ass nigga is talking about," Hassan lied to his wife. I looked at Hassan like he was deranged. It was one thing to lie to keep your wife, but this nigga was trying to play me.

My mind went blank. I slowly walked closer to Handle and grabbed his gun from his hand. I pointed it at Hassan. "Well, since we're proving our love to the ones we love babe, this nigga don't mean shit to me." I put the gun to Hassan's head and pulled the trigger. I pulled the fucking trigger, and his brains were all over the walls. I had no idea what I just did, but it was done. The room got quiet for a second and then his wife jumped on me. She grabbed my neck so hard I thought she snapped it. I was still in a state of shock from shooting Hassan, and I had to get out of it quick. His wife had the best of me until I came back to my senses. I fought her off for about six seconds until I heard another gunshot. Before I knew it, she dropped to the side of me. Handle had shot her. I stared at him as he stared at me. At that moment, I realized that I had my man back. I saw it all in his eyes, we were locked in again. This wasn't the first time we were in a murder scene together, but this was the first time we were killing together.

My mind was completely gone, and I was still in a state of shock. I had just killed a man. I've never killed anyone in my life. Handle grabbed me and shook me out of my frozen state. "Slim, snap the fuck out of it, we have to go!" Handle was shaking me and talking to me at the same time. I slowly came back to it and realized we surely did have to go. We were in a room with two dead bodies. Before I knew it, more men were walking into the room cleaning up the mess we had made. Handle grabbed my coat, grabbed my arm and we quickly left. We took the stairs instead of the elevator and exited the motel as quick and discreet as possible. Before I knew it, we were in my car and on the road, as if nothing happened. Handle was the driver this time. I replayed the night's events in my head and never imagined that this was how it would end. I had killed Hassan. I thought Handle was going to be the only one taking lives. I looked over at him and he was already looking at me while trying to stay focused on the road. "You alright?" He asked me. His voice was different, it was back to normal. He was talking to me as if I was Slim now instead of Naomi. I was happy inside. "Yes, babe I'm good," I answered. "Why'd you kill him?" Handle's question threw me off. Why did I really kill him? Was I mad that he was denying me to his wife? Or was I really trying to prove a point to Handle? I think I killed him for Handle but also for me. "I killed him because he was in the way of you loving me the way you were supposed to. You were

questioning my loyalty. You were questioning my

life and you were questioning my soul. I don't

like that. There's no Slim without Handle, and

there's no Handle without Slim. We ride

together we slide together," I meant every word

I said to him, and I hoped he knew. He didn't

say a word. He just smiled at me. I knew his

smiles. He was happy for us to be back where we

belonged. I promised myself I would never step

out on him again, and I also promised that I

would never let him step out on me again either.

A bitch was gone die next time! And I put that

on my soul. A nigga in love may be crazy, but a bitch in love that could take a life was almost the same match. We drove off holding hands and even deeper in love.

To Be Continued...

EVE'S BODY

It was an unusually cool day in late August as Eve sat in her all white 09 G37. Her lunch break was just starting, and already she'd lost the nerve to eat. Sweating profusely, her hands began to tremble as she looked down at what appeared to be a positive pregnancy test. She held back tears as a million and one emotions and memories flushed her body, causing her to rock back and forth. At this moment, looking like a psych patient to strangers walking past her car didn't matter, as she was suffering from an anxiety attack. *Bitch, calm down!* Eve slapped herself, trying to get it together. Breathing slow and deep the trembles lessened and the sweating stopped. Eve had become an expert over the years at calming herself, but she hadn't suffered from an attack in a long time. *How the fuck am I pregnant?* She asked herself out loud, knowing that it was damn near impossible. How am I going to tell Body? Still thinking to herself she jumped as her loud cell phone rang, startled her. Looking through the suitcase that she called her purse for her phone, she almost missed the call. It was Body. Nervous, Eve looked around at her surroundings, now caring what was going on. Her man was the type to pop up on her, so she wanted to be on point. "Hey baby," she said, finally answering the phone before the last ring. Her voice was so soft and sexy that it was unnoticeable that she had just been under pressure.

"I know you're hungry, I know you're tired, so take the rest of the day off and park your car in the garage. I'm coming to get you." Body didn't ask, he told Eve in his deep voice, and he wasn't taking no for an answer. He knew his girl was working extra hard lately on this new project she had going on and he just wanted some of her time.

"I can feel you, stop smiling so hard and hurry up," Body demanded as he

215

hung his phone up. He was a few minutes away from seeing his girl and he was excited. Eve couldn't close her mouth. Smiling from ear to ear, she threw the test in her glove department and fixed her face up. After throwing on some fresh eye liner and a fresh layer of lip gloss, she was ready to see her man. Already one of the prettiest brown skinned women around, it didn't take much for her to look great.

"You're all I need to get by, " by Mary J Blidge blasted through Eve's speakers as she started her car. This was her jam, turning it up higher she began to sing

along as she thought about Body. He was the second-best thing that had ever happened to her, but she found it so hard to show him. Knowing that he deserved all of her, past pain and hurt made it almost impossible for Eve to fully surrender, and now here she was pregnant. It had been a long time since she'd been in love, and even though the past two years with Body had been wonderful, trusting him was a struggle. The feeling of *'too good to be true'* always overpowered Eve's thoughts of him. Closing her eyes and smiling, in her mind she pictured the future with

Body and a new baby boy. She knew that one thing he always made clear was that he wanted children…all Kings, he would say. Whenever the conversation would come about Eve would always agree, but she knew that she probably could never give him what he wanted. Pushing all thoughts of babies and pregnancy tests out of her mind, she parked her whip and waited for her love to pull up. Body always surprised her with wonderful things, and she was anxious to see what this one was going to be.

The sound of HOV's voice poured through the streets and Eve knew it had to be her Mr. Almost Perfect pulling up. JayZ was his favorite rapper and sometimes all he played. Excited and a little horny, Eve jumped out of her car so that she could be the first thing he saw when he turned the corner. Eve was a bad bitch, and she felt like one just as much as she knew it, and just as much as she showed her nigga. It took her a long time to gain the confidence to realize her worth, and she used it well. Standing at 5' 7" tall, Eve had legs for days. They were tight, firm, and thick. The saying thick thighs save lives could've been created for her. Smooth Reese's brown skin covered her curvy body and complimented her big bubbly, hazel eyes. Looking like a black Rapunzel, honey brown hair laid down her back, stopping just above her apple shaped ass. Often mistaken for being mixed, Eve was 100% black and a little "ghetto" if you asked her. Full, plump lips covered her straight white teeth, giving her a smile to die for with deep dimples in both cheeks. Truly beautiful, Eve's face could melt hearts. A shiny black x6 with tinted windows turned the corner and pulled up like the driver owned the block. It was Body in a big boy. Happy to see his bitch he stepped out of his car with open arms. Eve ran to him as she always did and squeezed him like she missed him. Body held her extra tight and much longer than normal, as if he knew she needed a hug. "What's up pretty?" smiling hard he was admiring his shorty. She was perfect in his eyes. He felt that there was so much more to her that she wouldn't give him access to, but he was willing to wait. Knowing that she had been hurt before, he was patient with Eve. He honestly felt that she was worth it.

"Nothing much babe, I missed you," Eve whined while pouting and poking her lips out like a spoiled child. Body leaned forward and kissed her. "Well, daddy's here now. Let's go," Body's deep masculine voice sent comforting chills down Eve's back. Sounding so secure, his voice calmed her hysteria. Walking to the passenger side of his car Body opened the door for Eve to get in. Loving the way he treated her, Eve smiled as she hopped into the front seat. His beige leather seats were cool on her skin as the cold air from the AC crept through the vents. Sitting back and inhaling as she took a deep breath, Eve felt like everything was okay. Looking out of the rear-view mirror, she wondered why Body hadn't made it to his side yet. *The car ain't that big nigga* Eve giggled as she spoke out loud to herself. Body was standing with his back towards the trunk of the car having a conversation on the phone. Nosey as always Eve cracked her window so she could hear.

"Yeah...aight yo! I'll be there," Body's voice had tension in it as he hung up the phone. Quickly, Eve rolled her window back up before he could turn around. Her mind began to over think things. *Who the fuck was he arguing with? Where does he think he's going? Talking 'bout I'll be there, be where nigga? I really wonder what bitch he is beefing with…talking about aight yo. This nigga is funny.* Eve's thoughts were running so crazy, she didn't realize that Body was back in the car. "Calm down Eve, relax," Body spoke softly. He seen the worry all over her. *Damn, now he knows I'm bothered*, Eve thought to herself. "I am

calm, what you talking 'bout babe?"
Eve's soft voice was almost
convincing, but by now Body knew his
woman. She faked a smile as she put
her seatbelt on. "Oh okay, so you don't
need to check my phone to see who I
was just talking to?" Body asked
sarcastically. Eve laughed hard. She
couldn't hold it in, he just knew her too
well. "Nah it's cool, I don't need to do
all of that," Eve lied to him, and to
herself. She didn't need to, but she
wanted to, and it was a want that was
so hard for her to let go. "Here," Body
looked at Eve with an *it's fine crazy*

take it face and it made her smile. "I mean, if you want me to then I will," Eve joked while snatching the phone from him playfully. Right away, she went to recent calls and saw that the last call was from his sister, Bianca. Knowing he was watching her; she still clicked the details of the call to make sure the times added up. Still unsatisfied, she checked the details of the call under Bianca's contact info. Everything seemed valid. It made sense to Eve that he'd be arguing with Bianca, she was your typical spoiled baby sister.

"Are you done yet?" Body joked. He knew that Eve had enough problems, and he didn't want to be another one. He smiled at her as she handed him back his phone "Shut up," Eve laughed. "Mm hm," Body smirked as he pulled off. Suddenly stopping, he pulled over and put his car in park. Soft but firmly grabbing Eve's face, and looking deep into her eyes, he spoke with a serious voice "E, I got you shorty, you good with me. I'm not one of the bad guys. I'm not whatever his name is. That's my word on everything. You're mine and you see how I treat

227

what belongs to me. I know a nigga
done looked you in your eyes and lied
before, but I'm sure his actions weren't
the same. I'm showing you more than I
tell you and I'm waiting for you, but I
need to know that I'm getting
somewhere. Them niggas that fucked
up were either plain stupid or just
inexperienced. I've been around, I
know what's out there. You're a rare
one, and I ain't trying to lose
that." Body spoke. Holding back tears,
Eve smiled. So many words were on
her heart and tongue, but she couldn't
open up. Believing him was easy but

letting go of her past was her issue. "I have to tell you something," Eve's voice became worried. She wasn't sure if this was the time to tell him or if she should even tell him, but it was too late. "I'm pregnant," she blurted out before he could ask what it was. She had gotten it off her chest. Speechless, Body stared at Eve. Looking her body up and down from head to toe, pausing at her stomach, he smiled. Still quiet, thoughts of Eve in a wedding dress flooded his mind. She was his family now. "I love you, you're giving me my first king," body spoke. Eve felt the

sincerity in his voice. He placed his
hand over her stomach and replied,
"It's just us now," and smiled. As much
as Eve wanted to be ecstatic, she
wasn't. Deep down she knew that this
had to be a mistake. She couldn't give
him children. Looking at Body's
beautiful black face and perfect white
smile, it was so hard to disappoint him.
As always, she went along with it.
Smiling hard now, she raised her hands
and yelled out, "Surprise." Eve kissed
him deeply, trying to change the vibe.
Knowing Body knew her well, she
didn't want him to see her worry.

Body couldn't resist Eve's juicy lips on his tongue. He knew she was trying to take his mind off the baby news, but it didn't bother him. He wanted to fuck her even more now that she was carrying his seed. He kissed her back harder as she pushed him back in his seat. She wanted to be in control, and he liked it. Kissing his neck softly she rubbed his dick print through his sweats. It was firm and at attention. Lifting his T-shirt with her mouth she licked him from his neck down his chest to his groin. Her favorite thing about his Tommy boxers was the hole that you could slip the dick through. Taking his penis out she rubbed it with the side of her face and then with her soft hands. Body let out a moan that turned Eve on. She put her mouth on it closed her eyes and went to work. She gave her man head with her ass up in the air in the middle of the day, in the car, on a Brooklyn corner. She was like that, and he loved it. "I wanna cum all on your pretty face," Body was vulnerable during sex and Eve loved it. "Cum all on my face daddy, make a mess on it," Eve begged him to cum as Body released a large amount of creamy cum all over her face as promised. Dripping from her eyes to her nose, to her lips, to her chin, she licked it off as much as she could. Eve was a freak butt, and Body brought it out of her. Their sex life was amazing, and it was one of his favorite parts of their relationship. He often joked that her pussy was so good because she's been hurt in the past. "Damaged women have great pussy," he'd say. What he loved most about his woman was her whole aura. She was a boss, she was independent, she was beautiful, and she knew what she wanted out of life. Losing his virginity at 13, Body was very experienced with women, and at the age of 35 he had never met anyone as dope as Eve. This was especially true considering how young she was. She was 27 with an old soul. Body smiled as he watched her lick his cum up. "Was it good?" he asked sarcastically.

"Tastes better every time," smiling seductively, Eve spoke as she sat correctly in her seat. They both laughed as Body's tires sped off Into the Brooklyn streets.

TWO WEEKS LATER

"Eve Passion, the doctor will see you now," the nurse called from the waiting room. She was anxious and nervous. She needed to confirm that she was pregnant. "Eve, both your blood and urine tests came back today and, they were positive. You are indeed pregnant. Now I'm going to write you a few prescriptions and send you for a sonogram. We need to see the baby's measurements," the doctor told her. Eve thanked her and left the office. She went into the room the nurse told her to wait in and put on the medical gown. Eve was confused but overjoyed. For years she was under the impression that she couldn't have children. This was a miracle for her. She entered the room and was instructed to lay down. She did as she was told. When they placed the cold gel and then the machine on her stomach, she cried. Her baby's heartbeat was strong. Suddenly, she wished that Body was there to share the experience, but she knew that her first visit she had to do alone. Now that it was confirmed, and she knew for a fact that she was pregnant, she was in awe.

She would have her man with her for every visit from here on out for sure. Eve was overwhelmed with joy and happiness. She was ecstatic. She cried happy tears. Her phone chimed and she saw that it was a text from her best friend, Kiyana. The text read, *bitch Tyrone is back!!.* Eve's mouth dropped as she read it.

4 YEARS EARLIER

EVE

"Leave a message," it was Tyrone's voicemail again. "What's up babe, its E. I know you're working. I just wanted to let you know that Dr. Billinger called, and she wants me to come in for some tests. No worries, it's routine, call me later. Love you," Eve ended the phone call. She knew that he was on a business trip and was more than likely busy. She checked herself out in the mirror one last time. She looked amazing. Her curly dyed black hair was straightened and fell down her back. Her dark eye liner under her hazel eyes made her look exotic. She was on her way to her fertility doctor, and she was anxious to receive good news. *"I prayed on this, so I know it's my time,"* Eve whispered out loud. It's been a year and a half since she'd been with Tyrone, and their relationship hadn't been the greatest. For some reason, Eve felt that if she gave him a child, things would get better. Two months ago, she came up with the idea to tell Tyrone that she was pregnant so she could see his reaction. To her surprise, he was ecstatic. Eve was happy. She had found something that would save her love. She fell head over hills for Tyrone from day one, and she couldn't see herself being with anyone else. As much as Tyrone did wrong, he made Eve feel like everything was right, but her love for him was a delusion. The only problem that was in the way of them starting a family was her not being able to get pregnant. She had lied to Tyrone just to see his reaction and now she was stuck. Over the past few weeks, she had been faking a pregnancy, and today she was ready for some good news. She was ready to actually be pregnant. Tyrone went on business trips once a month, so it was easy for Eve to hide her period. After learning Tyrone's travel pattern, she even researched ways to make her period come when she wanted it to. In her mind, she was making her relationship work. Tyrone was being so much more caring since she had lied to him, and she missed that in their relationship. She had to do what she felt she had to do. Walking out of the house they shared together, she jumped in her money green Lexus and headed to her doctor's office. "Eve Passion, the doctor will see you now," the secretary called through the window. "Here we go, "she murmured to herself as she walked to the back. "Hi Dr. Billinger, how are you?" asked Eve as she held her hand out for a shake. "I am fine Eve and yourself? How are you? And I mean really, how are you?" Dr. Billinger inquired, sounding concerned as she shook Eve's hand and looked her in the eyes. " Well, I'm good, I hope " Eve laughed out loud, but Dr. Billinger did not. "I mean is something wrong

Dr. Billinger? You wanna just tell me?

You don't seem too good yourself."

Eve was nervous, Dr. Billinger was not

her usual self, normally she had quite a

sense of humor, but not today. "Eve,

when was the last time you saw an

OB/GYN?" asked Dr. Billinger in the

same serious tone. "About six months

ago. Why Dr. Billinger? Just say it,

damn!" frustration was taking over

Eve. " Eve, you have Gonorrhea and

you had to have had it for a while

because it did damage to your insides.

Your fallopian tubes are blocked and

that's why you are having trouble conceiving. Your tissue is badly scared, you need to start treatment right away," Dr. Billinger gave it to her straight. She has always been the *tell it like it is* kind of doctor because she knew that health was important. She felt sorry for Eve knowing how excited she was to be able to have a baby. Looking her up and down, Eve showed no emotion. Dr. Billinger respected how she kept her character. " So, wait a minute. I have Gonorrhea. I can't have kids. That's what you're saying?" Eve was hurt, confused, and most of all she was embarrassed. Although she wouldn't let it show physically, emotionally she was dying inside. "Yes Eve, that's exactly what I'm saying. I'm sorry," Dr. Billinger was lost for words and actions. She wanted to hug Eve, but she did not want to cross the professional line. Instead, she offered an ear. "Listen Eve, I have a heart outside of my job, take my number and call me. I don't want to be in your business and I'm not trying to be your mom but call me if you ever need to talk." Dr. Billinger wrote down her personal number on her card and handed it to Eve. "Thank you," was all that Eve could say as she took the card and left the room. She was numb and confused. She needed to be by herself. Dr. Billinger watched her leave the room as she felt even more sorry. She was so young and was dealing with a stress that was heavy. Dr. Billinger thought about her own daughter. Her thoughts changed quickly as she felt the tears forming. Pushing everything that just occurred to the back of her mind, she paged her secretary to call in her next patient.

Eve sat in her car and stared blankly out the window. She had no feelings. She had no one to call. She was numb and she was stuck. *She said I had Gonorrhea, gonofuckinrrhea, did y'all hear that shit? I can't have kids. A doctor told me that I have gonorrhea and I can no longer have children. Do you hear how crazy that shit sounds?"* Eve spoke to herself as If she was having a conversation and was waiting for a response. *"Relax Eve, relax, maybe this is a mistake"* she tried to sound convincing as she thought of the odds of the doctor being wrong. She knew that a mistake like this was very unlikely, especially from Dr. Billinger. Confused and numb, all Eve could do was cry. She could not understand for the life of her how or why this was happening. She just knew her and Tyrone were going to start a family. "This mother fucker!" Eve became angry again. "This mother fucker Tyrone! Is this nigga crazy?" Eve grabbed her phone and dialed his number. No answer. She continuously called his phone, becoming more and more angry every time he did not pick up. Her tears turned to loud cries and eventually screams. Throwing her arms like she was fighting to win; she punched her steering wheel until her fist hurt. *"I hate this nigga, I hate this motherfucking nigga,"* she pulled her own hair as she screamed these words from her heart. She hated him and most of all, she hated herself because she knew she still had love for him. All cried out, she started her car and drove…with no destination in mind.

TYRONE

"Damn," Tyrone spoke out loud when he realized that he had fallen asleep. Looking over to his side he saw his shorty still knocked out. They had just had wild nasty sex and it put both of them to sleep. Jumping up out of bed, Tyrone threw on his boxers and reached for his phone. He moved his shirt and pants and couldn't find it where he had left it. *"Am I tripping?"* he thought out loud, looking over to the dresser. His phone was lying face down on the dresser and Tyrone wondered if he had really forgotten where he put it. He was drunk last night after celebrating, but he would have bet money that wasn't where he placed it. Thinking nothing of it he checked his calls and messages. Of course, Eve would be one of the top five missed calls. He took a deep breath as he looked over at his shorty sleeping. Her stomach was round like a basketball, holding their son. *I don't know how Ima tell Eve this,* every time the thought came to Tyrone he felt like shit. He loved Eve so much. Her love took care of his soul. It was what every man needed. Now she was finally pregnant. But his shorty Clarice spoke to his demons. She woke up the wild side in him and they had a great time. He would always fantasize about her having his baby and now here they were. The only thing that saved Tyrone was the fact that Clarice lived in another country. Tyrone had met her while on a business trip in The Dominican Republic. She was the plug's first cousin, but they were close like siblings, so Tyrone had to be careful with her. They took care of their people, and they didn't tolerate disrespect of their women.

Clarice was beautiful. She was a Caramel-skinned Dominican with Asian eyes and long curly jet-black hair. Her skin was as smooth as a baby's ass and her smile was as bright as the sun. Her heavy Dominican accent turned Tyrone on whenever she spoke. Her breasts were plump and perky, and her ass was round and juicy. Clarice had some of the best pussy Tyrone had ever felt and tasted. She was beautiful and addictive inside and out, just like her country and just like its drugs. Being here with Clarice was like being in a trance for Tyrone. It was wrong because of Eve, but it felt so right. Now that they were having a baby, Clarice had been heavy on Tyrone's back about moving to DR for good. She was not willing to raise her first child with a seasonal father, as she would say. Tyrone had her under the impression that his mother was sick back home and that's what was stopping him. Clarice was no fool, she knew he had to have some type of intimate life but now she was giving him his first child. She was taking charge and everyone else had to fall in line, so she felt. "Babe wake up,"

Tyrone gently tapped Clarice's shoulder to wake her up. "I'm up babe what's wrong," Clarice's sleepy accent warmed Tyrone's penis veins. "Nothing is ever going to be wrong my love, are you and little man hungry? Let me feed y'all before I dip," Tyrone ended his statement with a kiss to her forehead. "Your little king is always hungry, let's eat," Clarice was always down for food. Her appetite was out of the world since she had become pregnant. She loved the way Tyrone cared for her and their child's well-being, weather he was miles away or right beside her. Whenever she called, he answered. "I don't want you to leave us, when is everything going to be fine with your mother? I want you here with us. It's getting closer to our king's arrival," Clarice laid down her begging voice and face to the fullest. She knew how to touch Tyrone's soft side and make him give in. "I'm tired of you leaving me daddy, I need you and papa here with me in the middle of the night," Clarice rubbed Tyrone's penis through his pants. Papa was a nick name she gave it. He was instantly turned on. Clarice always knew how to do it to him. "Don't worry babe I'll be back before you know it," Tyrone kissed her on her nose, trying to quiet her. "No papi, I'm tired of hearing that. I need to know what's going on. I don't wanna be waiting and worrying. The doctor says this stress isn't good for the baby." Clarice was putting an unusual amount of pressure on Tyrone. She was usually good with some bomb dick and great food, but not this time. Tyrone looked at her a little worried. "Listen C, I don't want you stressing my son out. Daddy is coming home. Haven't I been here?" Tyrone asked Clarice for reassurance. "Yes, papi but…" Clarice tried to cut him off, but he stopped her. "But nothing, I've been here, and I'll be here. I don't know if it's your hormones, but you better calm ya little ass down. I'll be back soon," Tyrone was stern. He didn't know what got into her, but it was unusual. He kissed her on her lips as a way of apologizing for raising his voice. "Just chill baby, I got you," he smacked her on her ass as he headed out the door. Clarice watched him leave. *"Yeah, I bet you will be back mother fucker,"* speaking to herself, her voice turned angry as her eyes almost burned a whole through the door.

KIYANA

Kiyana looked at the screen of her phone, trying to decide what to do. She had six missed calls from Eve, and she wasn't sure why Eve would have been calling. The last time she had spoken to her best friend, she had accused her of being jealous and told her to mind her fucking business and stay out of her relationship with Tyrone. All she was trying to do was tell her some shit

Tyrone was doing. Kiyana learned from that experience that if someone is dickmatized nothing can compete with that. She missed her friend so much, but she couldn't respect how she had let a man come in between them. They did everything together and were more like sisters than anything else.

Puzzled, Kiyana called Eve back. "Ki, I need you Ki, I'm so sorry," Eve was hysterical when she answered. "Eve calm down, what's wrong with you? Where you at?" Kiyana became worried. She instantly began to regret missing those six calls. "I'm home Ki, please pull up," Eve sounded horrible. "I'm on my way," she replied as she hung up, grabbed her keys, and headed to her best friend's rescue. Eve was her sister and there wasn't a thing that she wouldn't do for her. Eve was the soft one between the two of them and Kiyana didn't like that people would sometimes take advantage of that. Eve had to get a backbone for herself, but Kiyana would still pop out for her if need be. As she approached the door to leave, she decided to double back and grab her strap. She never knew what could come from Tyrone, and she knew that he had a hand problem. She wasn't with that. Now, ready for anything she jumped in her black Benz and sped to Eve's. Arriving to Eve's, the home they shared was a disaster. Anything that was glass was shattered, clothes were ripped up, bleached up, the couches were ripped. There was cotton and feathers everywhere. Kiyana looked around thinking the worse. The house was so bad she just knew something had to have happened to her friend. Suddenly, she heard cries from the back room. She pulled her gun out and ran to the

back, pointing it. She dropped her
weapon when she saw her friend sitting
on the floor crying while rocking back
and forth. She sat beside her and
hugged her long and tight. Eve cried
even harder now. Kiyana didn't know
what was wrong, but she hugged her
friend and didn't let go. "I love you
Eve, whatever it is we gone get through
it," Kiyana meant her words. She hated
seeing her friend like this and she
wanted revenge on whoever was
responsible for this... "He's having a
baby. Tyrone is having a baby," Eve
chuckled through her cries as she said

this. It sounded weird coming from her mouth. Kiyana's stomach turned, to think she was crying over him made her sick. She loved her friend, but she hated her choice of a man. Speechless, she remained quiet and let Eve vent. "He's having a baby Kiyana. This nigga is in The DR living a double life. I spoke to the bitch and everything. They're in love Ki, they had a baby shower bitch. I saw the pictures," Eve let out a harder laugh. She was furious but she had to laugh to keep from falling apart. "Look at this shit," she blurted out while handing the phone to

Kiyana. Eve showed her everything that Clarice had texted to her. There were videos, pictures, text messages, dates, family events…this nigga was really living a double life. Kiyana couldn't help but notice how beautiful the girl was. "Damn Eve, and she ain't even an ugly bitch this time, I mean at least you'll have cute step kids," Kiyana and Eve both busted out laughing. Eve loved Kiyana for the way she made everything seem okay. Her heart was broken into a million pieces, and she still had a sense of humor. "I hate this nigga yo! What am I supposed to do?" Eve's laughs turned back into cries. She was hurting so bad, and she couldn't dare tell Kiyana the news the doctor had just given her. That was something she was going to take to her grave. Yes, Kiyana has witnessed every embarrassing moment Tyrone had put Eve through, but she felt that this one was too personal. At least for now. "Eve you don't wanna hear advice from me. So, I don't know what to tell you, but I'm here," Kiyana was serious. She couldn't sugar coat anything with her sister. She hated what she went through, and she couldn't deny that. "I

266

do wanna hear it bitch! Shit I need to hear it. I need somebody to slap me or something Ki. Since we've stopped talking shit has been so crazy. This nigga be doing good then boom, it's all bad. I don't know what else to do," Eve sounded like a lost little girl. Kiyana hated it. She understood that Eve loved her nigga, but she couldn't understand how or why she couldn't love herself more. Eve was beautiful from looks to vibes she could literally get any man she wanted if she left this nigga, but she was stuck.

"Eve, look at you. Look at yourself right now. Girl, ain't you tired of this? Aren't you tired of crying E? Aren't you tired of getting cheated on? Beat on? Lied to? Disrespected? This nigga does whatever he wants. I mean, he has literally done 'whatever' since y'all been together. He knows you gone take him right back. Don't get me wrong he helps out but FUCK THAT NIGGA! You been that bitch before this nigga and you letting him devalue you. You don't need him E, for nothing, and you know that. You let him violate and disrespect you as if you are a nobody.

Look at yourself in the mirror Eve. Are you not worth more than this corny bum shit? Are you not worth real genuine love?" Kiyana felt tears forming in her own eyes. She loved her friend so much and just wanted her to choose better. She remembered the days when she let a nigga play her and she's never been the same since. She wished she could just give Eve the strength that she had when it was time to leave a nigga alone. Eve was quiet and taking in everything Kiyana was saying. Tears were coming down her face like a waterfall and she was feeling everything her friend was saying. "You are beautiful Eve, and I am not just saying that bitch. You are an ill ass bitch; I just don't know why you can't see that. This nigga doesn't deserve you anymore. You have put your time into this shit already. Yes, I know that you put blood sweat and tears into him but fuck all that, fuck it all. It's time to put on your big girl panties and let this shit go. Let these hoes have him because I guarantee you that nigga gone wish he never played you. He ain't changing, let him ruin the next bitch's life, it's time you get yours in order." Kiyana hugged her friend as she cried. Eve didn't speak, she just cried until she couldn't cry anymore.

TYRONE

"Why the fuck she ain't answering the phone?"" Tyrone asked out loud, frustrated. He'd been calling Eve for over an hour, and she hasn't answered. He wasn't sure if he should have been mad or worried, this was unlike her. Even if he didn't answer when she blew him up, she always answered when he called back. *"Aight,"* speaking out loud again, he ended his last call to

Eve and put his phone away. He looked around the airport for his ride. His driver was unusually late, everything was just out of order. Almost ready to flip out, he saw his driver creeping around the corner. *"What the fuck,"* Tyrone mumbled as he walked towards the car. The driver must've seen the look on his face as he pulled up, he instantly drove faster when he spotted him out. Parking the car, he quickly jumped out. "Sorry boss, there was heavy traff…" Tyrone cut him off. "It's cool Ray, I don't even want to hear it," he spoke respectfully but sarcastically. He let it be known that he was not happy with his performance. Ray has been his driver for a while, and this was unlike him, but Tyrone was already in a bad mood. "Take me home," Tyrone commanded Ray with respect but no manners. As his job, Ray did what he was told. *Yeah, shit must be going bad for him*, Ray thought to himself, and he sensed Tyrone's energy. Everything about him was off and picking him up late must've added to his aggravation. *When you do wrong, things go wrong. Get it together my brother,* Ray spoke to Tyrone through his thoughts. He turned his music up and drove to his destination.

"Something isn't right," Tyrone whispered to himself as Ray pulled into the driveway. Tyrone felt a bad vibe. Just feeling that there was something wrong, he jumped out of the car ready to face the problem. Walking into his huge home he stopped before he got his foot into the door. There was broken glass everywhere and he was sure that someone had robbed him. Turning around, he jogged to his bushes by his driveway and grabbed his Glock 19 out of one of his many secret stashes. He

walked back into his home with his weapon cocked and ready. The thought to call Eve's name out crossed his mind, but he didn't want to alert anyone right away if they were still inside. He wanted a good view of what was going on. Walking around now, Tyrone could see that everything was broken. He went to his room to see if it was a robbery like he suspected. Sure enough, his jewelry boxes were empty and out on the floor. "Eve, Eve," alarmed now Tyrone screamed for his girl. He couldn't believe he was robbed and now he was sick to his stomach about not knowing where Eve was. She was pregnant and missing. "What the fuck is really going on right now?" Tyrone threw his hands on his head as he screamed out loud and walked in circles. Like a light bulb popped in his head, he ran to his closet and checked for his safe. It was gone. Furious, he rambled through a few more things before he left his house. "Ray, take me to the hood," Tyrone commanded his driver with fury in his words. Ray felt like some shit was about to go down but he stayed calm and drove as he was told. He checked the time on his phone before turning his music back up and hitting the parkway. Tyrone sat in the back of his car feeling like a complete idiot. He couldn't believe he was open enough to be robbed. He had no idea who it could have been, and it killed him that he couldn't find Eve. Momma Mary, Eve's mom popped in Tyrone's head, and he pulled his phone out. Her phone went straight to voicemail. He called again and got the same result. He thought harder as he stared out of the window. He was almost at his destination. Kiyana, Eves best friend popped in Tyrone's head next. He did not have the best relationship with Kiyana at all, but he knew if anyone cared about Eve it was her mom first and her best friend right after. He scrolled through old messages between him and Eve until he found Kiyana's number. Calling her phone, he took a deep breath and prepared to deal with her attitude. "Who this?" Kiyana answered her phone like she was one of Tyrone's homeboys. "Yo, it's Tyrone Kiyana, what's up with you?" Tyrone matched her energy and was respectful. "Ain't shit, how you get my number? What's going on everything good?"

Kiyana replied, sounding a little confused by his phone call. "Yo Kiyana, I don't know what's going on, I got your number from me and Eve's text messages. The house was robbed and damaged and I don't know where Eve is. I was taking care of business and I came back home to a disaster. I've been trying to reach her but I'm getting no answer. I'm worried now, I don't know what's going on. I thought that if anyone would have heard from her or knew anything, it would be you," Tyrone sounded like he was really worried about Eve. *Taking care of business my ass*, she thought to herself. "What you mean ya house was robbed? What the fuck? Ima call her! I'm on my way back from Jersey now. If anything, I'll pull up and we can figure this shit out," Kiyana tried to sound as worried as possible. Tyrone liked how concerned she was. "Aight, hit me," he hung the phone up and thought some more. He thought about telling Kiyana about the pregnancy, but Eve wanted to keep it between them only. It was hard for her to get pregnant, and she wanted to keep it to herself to be safe. He still couldn't understand what the hell was really going on. Pulling up on the block, Tyrone looked around at the same crack heads who have always been around. He was from the hood, but he would never move back. He left the block to some of his younger soldiers, and they were doing okay for themselves. "Pull up around the back and wait for me," Tyrone ordered Ray as he jumped out of his car. His feet hit the dirty pavement as his nose sucked in the dirty air. He felt right at home in the hood. "Uncle Ty, Uncle Ty, can I get a dollar?" The neighborhood kids ran up to him excited for money. He always handed out dollars to them when they asked with no problem. "Here you go kids, look both ways before crossing that street," he watched as they crossed the street to go to the corner store. "My man, what's up, what's up, what brings you outside today?" Tyrone's childhood friend Lance walked up on him and gave him a handshake as if he was happy to see him. "I'm outside for some bullshit Lance and you're just the man I'm looking for," Tyrone answered stern and serious. "Oh, so you call me for bullshit huh?" Lance joked. "Nah, I call you when I need shit done," Tyrone reassured him that he was a job handler and that he admired his work. Lance was about his respect, family, and his business. If anything came in the way of that, it was bad for whomever or whatever it was. "Some niggas ran in my spot while I was away and I think they grabbed Eve," Tyrone tried to finish speaking but Lance cut him off. "What the fuck you mean they grabbed Eve Tyrone? Don't play with me. Who the fuck got my sister?" Lance immediately turned violent. Tyrone knew this was going to happen and therefore he didn't deliver the news to him over the phone. Lance and Eve were really cousins, but they grew up under the same roof so to the streets they were siblings. "Do you think I would come down here and play with you like this nigga? I don't know what the fuck is going on. I came back to the house, saw that I'd been robbed, and Eve is missing. She's not answering my calls or anything. I don't even know where to fucking start to look for her. I'm waiting for Kiyana to get back from Jersey. We gonna try to figure this shit out. I know how you feel about

Eve Lance, I'm sick too. We gotta put some niggas on the hunt to listen out for any type of info," Tyrone spoke to Lance, but he wasn't sure if he was listening. He was starring off into space with a bad look in his eye. "I'm going on the hunt. All I know is nothing better be wrong with my sister," Lance walked off and got on his phone. Tyrone wasn't sure how to take his words and movements, but he didn't take it personal. He knew Lance would kill for Eve just as much as he would.

EVE

"Tyrone called me. He fell for the robbery. He's really worried about you too," Kiyana spoke to Eve on the phone. "Fuck him! I hope he loses his mind trying to find me," Eve responded with hatred in her heart. "I lied and told him I was in New Jersey, and I'll pull up on him to help find you,", Kiyana started laughing. "He believed me too, I don't know how I'm supposed to sit around him and go along with this shit," Kiyana was still giggling as she spoke on the phone. "I don't know Ki, I ain't really think this shit through."

They both began laughing hard, realizing that they were always doing some dumb shit together. "Don't worry Ima figure shit out on this side, you just do what you gotta do," Kiyana became serious. Tyrone was the least of her worries. She wanted to make sure her friend was okay. Eve always tried to keep a game face on through all of her tough times, but Kiyana knew that deep down inside she was hurting. "Are you sure you're gonna be aight by yourself?" Kiyana asked a little worried. "You said put on my big girl panties, right? I'm always good Ki.

Thank you for everything…for real,"
Eve sincerely thanked her friend. "I
gotta go. I'll call you later. I love you,"
hating saying goodbye, Eve hung up
the phone before Kiyana could respond.
She didn't want to start being mushy on
the phone knowing that she was going
to miss her friend. She looked around
her hotel suite. "This is it ladies,", she
said to herself out loud. "This is our
home for a while." She took a deep
breath and felt uneasy. Her whole
world had changed in less than 24
hours, and she didn't know if she could
adjust. She missed Tyrone and wanted

him dead at the same time. She felt her heart begin to race and her hands start to tremble. *"Calm down Eve, roll up,"* she spoke to herself as she tried to relax. She took a few deep breaths and began to roll some weed up. After rolling three L's, she took her Bluetooth speaker out of her bag and played her music. She turned it up as loud as it could go and ran herself a bath in the suite's jacuzzi. Eve undressed as the tub filled up with hot water. She grabbed her lighter and ash tray and locked herself in the bathroom. She slowly stepped into the tub as the

hot water warmed her skin and then
blood. Sitting in the tub she took a long
deep breath and tears began to fill her
eyes as she got deeper into the water.
She couldn't control her feelings
anymore and they were forcing their
way out. She lit her first blunt and
smoked while she cried. All she ever
did was try to love Tyrone and she
couldn't understand how he could do
her how he did. Eve didn't know if the
Gonorrhea or the baby was worse. She
cried more thinking of how
embarrassed she was being told that
horrible news at the doctor's office, and

then having to get needles stuck in her ass. She cried more as she thought about the baby. She hit her L harder and harder as her thoughts took over. Pictures of Tyrone holding Clarice's stomach floated in her head as she replayed their conversation. Clarice told her so many things about Tyrone that it was literally sickening. Eve couldn't believe that another woman knew her man so well. It hurt her heart so bad to think of her soulmate sharing so much love with another woman. Eve's eyes were waterfalls, and her breathing was heavy, she was so deep into her thoughts that she didn't realize how much she had been crying. Getting out of the tub, she sat on the edge as she tried to relax herself. Rocking back and forth she continued to hit her blunt until she began to breathe easier. *"I love this nigga too much,"* Eve spoke out loud. *"I love this nigga too fucking much,"* Eve's voice began to crack as she cried and continued to speak out loud. "Look at me, look how this nigga got me" Eve was ashamed as if someone was personally watching her life. Still rocking back and forth, she replayed memories of her and Tyrone in her head as she smiled, laughed, and cried. She had been with Tyrone going on two years and shit was only getting worse. Eve knew she had to let this nigga go. *Even if she wanted to be with him, how could she?* She thought. She didn't know how she'd be able to forgive him for a baby. Wiping her face, she jumped up and grabbed a towel. *"Get it together bitch,"* she spoke to herself in the mirror. *"Fuck him."* She let her tub water out and turned the shower on. She changed her playlist from R & B to rap, then jumped in the shower. The hot water ran over her body as she closed her eyes. "Fuck him Eve, fuck him! we don't need him", she spoke to herself as her last few tears fell from her eyes. "You gone be good and that nigga gone feel you soon." She wiped her eyes and laughed. "I'm good." Feeling the rap lyrics coming through the speaker, Eve began to rap along. Within minutes her shower went from a crying well to a performance stage. She laughed at herself twerking in the shower and for the moment everything felt alright.

TYRONE

At the end of the night Tyrone sat alone in his room replaying his day over. Trying to figure out how he ended up where he was, he started remembering everything that was out of order. *"Why wasn't my phone where I left it?"* He asked himself in his head. *"why was my driver late?"* *"Where the fuck is Eve?"* He continued to question himself as his blood started to boil. Tyrone didn't like to be played with. He hated feeling like a fool. Thinking he jumped to conclusions about being robbed, he tried to think of who would or could really rob him. "There's no way I got robbed" speaking calmly to the dark room Tyrone tried to figure it out. Picking his phone up off the table he decided to call Kiyana. *"It's been enough time, she should be back, this was an emergency,"* he thought. Kiyana's phone rung twice and went to voicemail. He called again and it did the same. Feeling funny, he knew something was up. *"Fuck me being robbed. Eve Is missing and you haven't hit me,"* Tyrone thought to himself as he began to get angrier. His blood was heated and boiling. His demeanor was relaxed but inside there was a war going on with his demons. He called Clarice. "Hey baby what's up?" She answered on the first ring like most times. "How's my son?" Tyrone asked. "He's up moving around as always...hungry," Clarice rubbed her stomach as she spoke. "How's my baby momma?" Tyrone asked as he thought about his words. *Damn* he thought to himself *"Eve is missing and I gotta baby moms."* His thoughts were bothering him more and more. "My feet are swollen daddy. I wish you were here to rub them. It's like I'm getting

bigger by the minute. I'm huge,"
Clarice whined. "Don't worry, daddy
will be there soon to take care of all of
that. What you doing though?" Tyrone
asked. "Watching Eve's Bayou,"
Clarice answered. "What you just say?"
Tyrone's anger surfaced and startled
Clarice. "Looking at these bottles, God
damn baby what the hell you thought I
said?" Clarice was upset. She was
pregnant and emotional and did not like
how he yelled at her. Tyrone took a
heavy deep breath. "Nothing yo, I gotta
go. I love y'all," Tyrone hung up the
phone. He thought he heard her say

Eve's name. His mind was tripping now and he started feeling guilty about his sin. *"This is crazy,"* he thought to himself. The last person he decided to call was Lance. " Yo," Lance answered, sounding bothered. "What's up yo? You heard anything yet?" Tyrone asked, hoping he'd get some answers or at least some hints. "Nah I didn't," Lance spoke as if he didn't want to speak. "Damn, you good?" Tyrone asked sensing Lance's vibe. "Nah I'm not good. But when I hear something, trust me mother fuckers gone know" Lance made a solid statement that he meant. "I feel you bro," Tyrone tried to understand. "Nah nobody feels me yet," Lance spoke again, short but powerfully. "I'll hit you though, and you let me know something soon," Lance instructed before he hung up. Tyrone looked at his phone and felt some kind of way. He understood how close him and Eve was, but he didn't like how Lance was moving and talking. Tyrone felt that he wasn't an enemy so he shouldn't be treated like a suspect. He thought more. *"I guess shit is different depending on who you are to a person. I respect that,"* Tyrone thought to himself as he got up and went to try and get some sleep.

CLARICE

Clarice sat in her brand-new rocking chair that Tyrone had put together before he left. It was one of their favorite gifts, and she thought about how excited he was to say that he was going to use it. She had been sick since Tyrone left. Pretending as if nothing was wrong almost killed her, but

Tyrone fell for her act. Rubbing her pained stomach as she rocked back and forth, she thought about her encounter with Eve on the phone. The man she was in love with belonged to someone else. Eve told Clarice that she and Tyrone were married and had a set of boy and girl twins. Clarice's heart has been hurting ever since, and she was lost. She knew that it was impossible for him not to be sleeping with anyone with their distance, but she never expected him to have a family. She couldn't eat or sleep and it was starting to bother the baby. He wouldn't sit still at all, and it made her nerves worse. Clarice hated Tyrone with everything in her. She loved her baby but hated feeling a piece of him inside of her moving. She felt disgust and love at the same time. *"This nigga ain't shit,"* Clarice told herself as she cried. Still re-playing their conversation, she thought about everything that Eve had told her. There was a part of her that wanted to hate Eve, and a part of her that felt bad for her. *"Niggas ain't shit,"* Clarice thought to herself again. She thought about how he had told Eve that he was on business trips whenever he was with her. *Business trips,* she thought as she let out a little giggle. *"So that's all this was to him?"* Clarice asked herself in her head. *"There is just no way. This nigga is always so happy when he's here with me and he treats me so good. Maybe he loves me more than Eve and he just doesn't know how to leave his family. Damn! Should he leave his family? I mean, I'm his family now too. Eve is in the way of us."* Clarice's thoughts took over her mind. Beyond confused and emotional, she cried. Her hormones were all over, and she couldn't control her tears. She began to breath heavy, and she started to feel uncomfortable as the baby pressed harder and harder against her stomach. "Ok hijo, calmarse pappi," Clarice spoke in Spanish to her son, telling him to calm down. "Mamá vienen aquí rápido," she called out for her mother. "Sí mamí?" Her mom answered right away. "Algo está mal con el bebé. Llamar a la abuela." She told her mom that something was wrong, and she should call her grandmother who was also her midwife. Clarice's family did not believe in hospitals or most doctors.

Most of the babies born in their family were born at home and delivered safely. This was Clarice's first child and she wanted to do everything her grandmothers did. Her mother hurried to get help. Clarice continued to rub her stomach as she watched knots form through her skin. Suddenly a trickle of water flowed down her leg, and she thought that maybe she had peed on herself. Great grandma Nelli, as the family called her, barged into the room to check on Clarice. She saw that she was sweating uncontrollably. "Baby, what's the matter?" Grandma Nelli spoke English as well as other languages, but her heavy accent sometimes made it hard for others to understand. "I don't know mama, look!" Scared as ever, Clarice lifted her night gown over her stomach to reveal what the baby was doing. Grandma Nelli smirked. "It may be time," she spoke softly to Clarice as she gently grabbed the rosary beads that hung around her neck. "But mama, I have six weeks to go," Clarice responded in a worried tone. She thought about Tyrone. She thought about bringing her first child into the world without his father. Tears began to fill her eyes again. Grandma Nelli noticed how distraught Clarice was. She closed the door and sat next to her, rubbing her back. "Child, I'm not going to ask you again what the matter is." Grandma Nelli gave Clarice the "look" that represented a stern warning. Clarice's eyes watered more. She couldn't tell anyone what Tyrone did. She was too embarrassed, and she didn't want her family to exile him. They did not take kindly to the disrespect of their women. She knew that she could trust great grandma Nelli with her life, but she was still uneasy about telling anyone. Thinking everyone would judge her and try to interfere, she went against her nerves and told her grandma. "Mama Nelli, I'm just scared. I'm nervous. I don't know what's going to happen. My hormones are all over and I'm just stressed." Clarice was being honest with Mama Nelli, she was just keeping her heart out. Her Heart was hurting badly, so bad, but she wouldn't speak about it. "Baby you will be fine. The best thing that could ever happen to you is happening. You are about to bring a child into this world. Nothing else matters. Don't let anything or anyone interfere with the connection between you and your blessing. Everything you're taking in and feeling right now is passing through him. Be easy baby girl, you're in the most beautiful stage of life. You must understand that and breathe easy," Grandma Nelli's words warmed Clarice's spirit. It was as if she knew something that she wasn't telling her. Clarice sat quietly with her eyes closed, breathing as grandma Nelli continued to rub her back. She called out for one of the butlers to come run Clarice a hot bath with floral water. Grandma Nelli took Clarice's night gown off and walked her to the tub, helping her to get in. "You sit in here and relax. Think about what you want to do with your son when he gets here and as he gets older." Grandma helped Clarice to relax and almost come back to herself. "Thank you , I love you." Clarice was thankful for her grandmother. "Child hush and connect with that baby. After the bath we can call Tyrone and let him know what's going on." Grandma Nelli instructed as she left the room and closed the door behind her. Her words lingered in the room behind her hitting Clarice's nerve. She pushed all thoughts of Tyrone, Eve and their family out of her head as she did what her grandma said. She spoke softly, out loud to her stomach while rubbing it, "I'm sorry pappi. I don't want you to feel no worry or pain. Mommy loves you so much. You are being born a king. Daddy is a piece of shit but we're going to be fine." She closed her eyes as she continued to speak to her baby while rubbing her stomach.

KIYANA

Kiyana popped another perc and realized she needed to slow down. She loved being high, it took her mind off of her lonely heart. *"Let me call Clue and see what his ass is doing,"* she spoke to herself as she scrolled through her text messages to find Clue's number. Clue was Kiyana's favorite fuck buddy, but he was also her best friend. All the other niggas she dealt with meant nothing to her. The first man she gave her heart to had broken it, and he died before she could ever get closure. This made Kiyana's heart cold, she never wanted to get attached to another soul. Clue was different, he was her best friend before the sex and the sex only made their relationship better. He was the closest to love that Kiyana felt she would ever get.

"What's craccin Kiki?" Clue gave Kiyana this nick name when they started messing around. He was in a gang known as "The Crips" and he was proud of it. He spoke it, he wrote it, and he lived it. "What you doing nigga, where you at?" Kiyana was glad he answered. She felt lonely for some reason and needed company. "I could be doing you," Clue laughed "I'm coolin. What's up?" he asked her. "Roll up," Kiyana said as she smiled. He knew what she really meant, the drugs were kicking in and she was horny. "Aight, I'm coming," Clue hung up and Kiyana got herself together, waiting for her dick appointment to arrive.

Clue thought about his friend after hanging up his phone. He loved Kiyana to death, but he wished that he could give her more, she deserved it. He knew she was afraid of love and was just settling for sex. He loved the pussy, but he loved her more. He wished that he could heal her heart. Kiyana was one of the toughest females he knew. She was like a nigga in a female body to him. She was fine as wine and was about her paper. He felt like her heart being broken was probably the worst thing that happened to her, she was a beautiful person, but the hurt made her attitude ugly. *Fuck it*, he thought, as he pushed the soft side he had for her to the side. He made a few more business moves before he got ready to go bust Kiyana's ass. Kiyana looked at herself in the mirror with her black lingerie on. Her hair was curled up and she looked good. She sprayed some perfume on her wrist, neck, and lightly on the inside of her thighs. Kiyana was dark skinned with slanted eyes and full lips. She had very dark eyebrows and curly lashes. She was well in her 20s and looked like a baby doll. Her petite figure complimented her round ass. She was no taller than 5'4, and she was a fun sized package If you asked her. She put on more eye liner and some lip gloss before she took two glasses out for drinks. She was ready for a good night with Clue. Her doorbell ranged and she cheesed hard.

She turned on some music before walking to her door to check the peep hole. To Kiyana's surprise, it wasn't Clue. It was Lance. She opened the door and went to her room to grab her robe. Lance watched her ass jiggle as she walked away and fantasized about having sex with her. He has longed for Kiyana since forever, but he didn't want to deal with any of his family's friends. "What's good stranger? What the hell are you doing here this time of night?" Kiyana was worried that something was wrong. "I guess you didn't hear about Eve," Lance got straight to the point of his visit. "Oh shit," she said to herself, they never ran the plan by Lance. Kiyana let out a little giggle before responding. "Ain't shit funny right now, I'm dead ass," Lance cut her off before she could continue. "Lance baby, relax. Eve is fine. She went on vacation. Call her," Kiyana was looking Lance up and down and her already warmed vagina became wet. All the pills she had popped were taking over and Clue was taking too long. "What you mean she's on vacation? This nigga Tyrone told me she's missing," Lance was beginning to get frustrated. He didn't think any of this was a game. "Fuck that nigga, Tyrone. He is the reason she's gone. Just call Eve, she'll tell you everything. We set it up to look like someone robbed him. Fuck him," she added. Lance was confused but at ease that he knew Eve was okay. Seeing how high Kiyana was, he didn't think it was a good time to ask her more questions about the situation, so he took his phone out to dial Eve. He called three times and each time her phone went straight to voicemail. Same thing it had been doing. He looked at Kiyana again, wondering if she was lying. He gently put his hand around her neck as he spoke softly in her ear. "You better not be lying with ya sexy ass," He licked her cheek and then kissed her nose. "Oh, I'm sexy?" Kiyana was turned on by his grip on her neck and the words that he whispered to her. She flirted back with him, letting him know that it could go down right then and there. "You know you sexy. I wanna stick my dick in you," Lance trolled her some more. Kiyana was soaking wet and wanted to spread her legs open right there but she knew that Clue was on the way. She wanted Lance, but no nigga came before Clue, plus…she wasn't sure if she was just horny and high. "I'll let you stick your dick in me whenever you want," Kiyana answered. She went right against her thoughts. She couldn't help herself. She loved sex and she needed it. Lance took her words as a green light and began to kiss on her. Kiyana kissed him back with no hesitation. Before she knew it, he had her pinned up against the wall with his face all in her pussy. She was on cloud nine. Lance's rough, thug tongue was so gentle and warm on her vagina. He sucked, licked, and ate her pussy like a full course meal. Kiyana came three times before Lance took her off the wall and laid her on the couch. Unbuckling his belt, he was ready to give her some dick. Kiyana came back to her senses after she nutted. *"I can't fuck him right now Clue is coming,"* she thought in her head. *"This nigga's dick is so big though,"* she was so confused about what to do. "Lance we can't do this right now," Kiyana spoke softly. "What? You just got your nut off right. You gone give me some pussy," Lance wasn't taking no for an answer. He grabbed her legs and threw her on her back. "Nigga chill out," she sat up on her arms beginning to get alarmed. "Get off of me," she pushed him and jumped up. Lance realized that she was serious and a little scared. "Damn ma, chill. I just thought you liked a little rough role play," Lance didn't mean to make her uncomfortable. "Nah I do, it's just…not tonight," Kiyana looked at the clock on the wall. It was well passed an hour and she just knew Clue would be pulling up any minute. "We can finish this tomorrow…me, you and him," Kiyana tapped his dick and made it jump. "Ima make it up to y'all," Kiyana put on her innocent look and it made Lance's dick even harder. "We gone hold you to your words too," he kissed her on the lips and then left the house the same way he came in. He surely was going to come back.

On his way out he felt like somebody was behind him. He turned around, but no one was there. Lance was a real street nigga and he had great street sense. He walked in the direction that he had sensed someone, but still saw nothing. Hearing a garbage can move behind him, he quickly turned around with a gun pointing. All he saw was a cat. *I know I ain't slippin,* he thought in his head as he looked around one last time before getting in his car and pulling off.

Kiyana took a deep breath, thinking about what had just occurred. Lance's head was amazing and she was so anxious to hump on him. Still wondering where Clue was, she jumped in the shower to freshen herself up. She put on a new lingerie set and fixed her curls before rolling up a blunt and poppin another perc. "Ok now Clue, I

could've been getting dick right now,"
she laughed as she spoke to herself.
"Fuck it Ima call him, "she said, as she
started dialing his number. There was
no answer. *Hmm*, she wondered. This
was unlike him, but maybe he was still
busy she thought.

TYRONE

Tyrone sat in his car heated. He
watched Lance pull off from Kiyana's
house and he knew that he was being
played. He couldn't sleep so he had
decided to pull up on Kiyana to see
what was going on, being that she

wasn't answering her phone. To his surprise he saw Lance. The fact that they were meeting up and Kiyana was ignoring him made him even more angry. He was confused and he didn't know what to do. He needed answers, he wanted to know where Eve was, and he wanted to know like yesterday. He sat in his car for a few more moments, deciding on whether to go to Kiyana's door. Not wanting to seem like a stalker, he decided against it. *Ima get her ass*, he thought to himself as he pulled off.

The next morning, Tyrone was up bright and early, ready to turn the streets up. He respected Lance and knew how he felt about Eve, but he still didn't like to be disrespected. He felt like Lance and Kiyana had one up on him and he didn't like it. He sat in his chair thinking long and hard, trying to think of anything that could lead him to Eve. Suddenly, Tyrone remembered that Eve had left him a voicemail. He never checked his voicemail. "What's up babe, its E, I know you're working but I just wanted to let you know that Dr. Billinger called and wants me to come in for some tests. No worries, it's routine, call me later. Love you!" Tyrone felt uneasy as he listened to Eve's voice on his speaker. He missed his bitch and was worried. The thought of something being wrong with Eve and his unborn was eating him alive, but he did a good job of covering it up. "Aight, let's call Dr. Billinger," he said out loud as he searched for the doctor's name on google. He was unable to find any OB with that name. The only Dr. Billinger that was coming up was a fertility doctor. *Well, I know she don't go to this doctor,* " Tyrone thought to himself. He was confused. He kept searching google and when no other doctor came up, he decided to just call the one he found. "Fertility in your Future, Megan speaking," a soft voice answered the doctor's phone. "Hi, I'm calling on behalf of my wife. I'm trying to find out if she's a patient of yours," Tyrone put on his professional voice. "I'm sorry sir, but that information is private, and I cannot disclose it over the phone," Megan's soft voice turned firm. "I understand. Is this Dr. Billinger's office?" Tyrone asked, making sure he was calling the right place. "Yes, sir, it is, is there anything else you may need help with?" Megan was getting a little impatient. "Sorry for the questions but would a pregnant woman be coming to this office to be seen?" Tyrone was confused. "Sir this is a fertility office, we help people who may have certain conditions that prevent pregnancy. So, most likely if you're pregnant and healthy already, this isn't the place for you." Megan was ready to hang up. "Thank you, Miss." Tyrone ended the call. Fed up, he was ready for mercy. Nothing was making any kind of sense to him and he was done with the games. As he went to make another call, his phone rang, and it was Clarice again. She had been calling the entire time he was speaking to the doctor, and he had no intention of calling her back. His mind was too wrapped up with Eve. *"Damn,"* he thought to himself as he thought about Clarice. He knew that she was due soon, and he started to feel like a fool for not answering. He called Clarice right back after he missed her call for the 10th time. "Hey baby," Tyrone tried to sound like he missed her, but his mind was occupied. "Don't hey baby me, why aren't you answering the phone?" Clarice's voice had aggravation, pain, and worry in it. Tyrone almost felt bad. "I was making moves baby, I'm sorry. What's going on? How's my boy? Are y'all alright?" Tyrone sound concerned and he was. Clarice wasn't sure how to feel. The trust that she had for him was gone and the love she felt for him was different. "It's time! He's coming, you need to get here as soon as possible Tyrone and I am not playing with you!" Clarice was as serious as she's ever been. "I'm on my way!" Tyrone hung the phone up and called his driver. He needed to find Eve, but he wasn't willing to risk missing the birth of his first son.

"Son," he thought to himself... "I'm having a son," he spoke out loud. Tyrone felt joy and sorrow at the same time. He was sharing life with someone other than Eve and he thought Eve was carrying his baby as well. Not a damn thing was making sense to him and although he wanted to get to the bottom of this, he needed to clear his mind. Going to see Clarice always provided peace of mind for Tyrone and this is what he needed now.

After making plans with his driver, he called an old friend of his from the hood, Tommi. Now Tommi was a benefit in many different ways, almost anything you needed you could get from her. She knew so many tricks of the trade that you'd never know all that she had going on. "T speaking, what's good?" She answered in her ratchet-toned voice. No matter how far she went in life she always kept a little spice about her. "Yo T, what's up sis? What's going on?" Tyrone sounded like he was speaking to a long, lost cousin. "Who the hell is this sis'n me?"

Tommi asked, unable to catch the voice on the other side of the phone. "Damn so a nigga number ain't stored no more? It's Tyrone yo," Tyrone spoke sarcastically. "Ohh shit! Hey Tyrone! What's up nigga? Where you been? Yo, you know I change my phones like I change my mind. I don't keep any old numbers." She spoke as if she was happy to hear from him. They went way back and were always cool. "Man, I'm around , where you been is the question," Tyrone giggled as he continued speaking. "I need to do some business with you. I heard you may be able to help me," Tyrone finished. "Oh yeah, and who did you hear that from? I'm always around, people just don't see me, what's up though? What type of business you talking? Come pull up on me." Tommi was all ears when it came to business because that meant money. She had four spoiled kids who somehow, some way always needed something. "Aight, you still in the same spot?" Tyrone asked, unsure. It was always hard to keep up with Tommi, she never sat still. "Nah, actually I'm not. Damn it's been that long huh? You can meet me at my shop. I still have

that. Call me when you're ready,"
Tommi finished her conversation with
Tyrone.

Tyrone hung up the phone and took a
deep breath. He was relieved that he
might be getting somewhere. Now he
could be less stressed when he went
home to Clarice, so he thought.

CLARICE

Clarice laid back as her contractions
began again. They weren't too bad, but
she knew they were going to get worse.

Her emotions were all over the place as she thought about her life. Everything had changed since she found out about Eve. Clarice felt crazy because she almost liked Eve, she almost felt her pain through the phone. She looked at her phone as she thought about texting Eve. The last time they spoke they came up with a game plan to get back at Tyrone. Clarice was all for it in the beginning, but now she was having mixed emotions. Being in actual labor, knowing that her son was entering the world had Clarice rethinking all her life choices. Did she really want to harm the father of her child? Unsure, she decided to text Eve anyway and keep her updated. *-HEY! LITTLE MAN IS ON HIS WAY! I'M SO NERVOUS & EXCITED!*

Eve texted her back, *WOW! HE'S COMING EARLY. HE MUST BE READY! LOL THIS IS A BEAUTIFUL MOMENT. RELAX AND ENJOY IT! IM HERE, KEEP ME POSTED! BLESSINGS ON A SAFE DELIVERY!*

Reading Eve's text made her emotional. She was trying to relax, she was trying to enjoy this moment, but her heart was confused. Clarice put her phone down and went back into thought. Her pain was easing, and she was tired. She drifted off to sleep rubbing her stomach.

TYRONE

As Tyrone sat on the plane, he thought about becoming a father. His first child and son was about to enter the world, and he couldn't wait to meet him. *"Am I man enough to raise a man?"* Tyrone thought to himself. He knew that a father held a great role in life, and he felt ready, but he was nervous. *"Do I give him my name? Or do I let him make one for himself?"* Tyrone's thoughts were non-stop. He wondered if his son would look more like him or more like his mom. He thought about Clarice, she was beautiful inside and out, he loved her without a doubt. He thought about Eve, she was beautiful even though she was damaged. She touched a part of Tyrone that he didn't know he had. He needed her no matter what else he had going on. He was conflicted because of his son. He was most important now, and he came with Clarice. For years he wanted children with Eve and now it was almost too late. Clarice was due. Tyrone felt a bad chill flow through his body when he thought about leaving Eve for his family. *"Where the fuck is*

Eve?" he asked himself. Right now, Eve was moving shady to Tyrone. His worry was turning into caution. Nothing was making sense and she was still nowhere to be found. Tyrone took a deep breath and leaned back in his seat. Closing his eyes, he tried to focus on his son. He pictured his own face on a baby and smiled. He breathed a little easier as he thought more about his son. Drifting off to sleep, he felt good knowing soon he would be holding his little man.

KIYANA

Kiyana sat on her couch thinking about Eve. She hadn't answered the phone since she left, and she had no exact location for her. She knew she was okay, but she just missed her friend. Bored, Kiyana flipped through her contact list to see who she could bother. She stopped on Clue's name. She hadn't heard from him since he stood her up. *"Nah, fuck him, he gotta call me first,"* Kiyana thought to herself. She put her phone down and decided to roll up. Being high kept Kiyana balanced, whether it was weed or pills, she needed something. She loved to mix it when she wanted to be wild, but she was just chillin right now, smoking would do her fine. After rolling, she lit her blunt and walked into her 'lady cave' as she called it. This was a room that very few people have been in, in fact, Kiyana has only let Eve & Clue in this room. She uncovered a piece of her recent artwork and sat down to finish working on it. Very few people knew that Kiyana was a dope ass artist. She could draw and paint her ass off. She never showed it off because it wasn't for show to her, it was therapeutic. As someone who suffered from anxiety, painting was the only thing she enjoyed enough to relax. Since she was a little girl, Kiyana has always enjoyed painting, both at home and in school, it kept her busy. As she got older, she put it off, but becoming an adult with her own home she knew that she needed it. It was the softest and most secret thing about Kiyana.

Boom, boom, boom, about 20 minutes after she started painting Kiyana heard an unusually hard knock on her door. *"Who the hell is banging on my damn door,"* she thought to herself. Walking up to her peep hole as she began to ask who it was, her door was kicked in on her and she hit the floor. "What the fuck?" she screamed out as she watched men dressed in all black run into her place. "Shut up bitch," she heard before receiving a hard kick to her face. She felt the blood rush from her nose. She couldn't beat a man, but she has certainly beat on enough females to hurt one. Trying to shake the shock off her spirit, she crawled up on to her knees. The same man kicked her again on her side, pushing her closer to the steps where she wanted to go. Kiyana coughed hard as his kick knocked the wind out of her. Reaching the bottom of her steps, she pushed her secret step and it opened, revealing her pink SR40c. Quickly, Kiyana turned around and shot the same man that hit her in his balls. "Arrrhhhh you dirty bitch!" the man screamed out as he pointed his gun at Kiyana, ready to pull the trigger. Instantly, another man came to where they were and shot the same man who was trying to shoot Kiyana, in his head. His body dropped like a fly. He then pointed his gun at Kiyana. "Put the gun down," he told her in a serious but calm tone. Kiyana put the gun down and the intruder kicked it away. "Get up, and go in your room," he gave Kiyana a firm order. Scared to death and and nervous, she did as she was told. Kiyana had more weapons stashed in her room, so she was glad to go there. "Clean your face off in the bathroom and come lay down on the bed," the intruder instructed. *"What the fuck kind of sick shit is this nigga on?"* Kiyana thought in her head. *"What the fuck is going on? Who are these people in my house? I can't believe he just killed someone in my living room. Oh my*

gosh I wish I would've called Clue!"

Kiyana's thoughts were running wild as

tears flooded her eyes. She had never

been more scared in her life. She

washed the blood and tears from her

face, then dried off with a towel. She

looked at herself in the mirror and

stopped crying. "You gonna be aight,"

she told herself before walking out of

the bathroom. "You like to pop pills,

right?" the intruder's voice was

sickening to Kiyana. It was so calm but

firm that it was nerve wrecking and

weird. "Take the pills on the dresser,"

he continued. Kiyana looked at him like he was crazy. "Listen, I don't know what you want from me but…" she began to plead as the intruder cut her off. "Where's Eve?" He was straight forward about what he wanted. Kiyana caught herself almost shaking, giving in to her nervousness. "I don't know where my friend is, she's probably somewhere with that no-good nigga of hers," Kiyana tried to play it off like she didn't know. The intruder cocked his gun back and pointed it at Kiyana. "Take the pills," he told her again. Kiyana's heart began to race.

She looked down at the pills and she had never seen them before. For all she knew, she could've been taking dope. She began to cry as she thought about her options, rat her friend out or stay solid. She would never in a million years be a snitch bitch, especially if it was her best friend she was telling on. *"God you've been with me through everything, I need you more than ever now. Please be with me while I take these drugs. Amen."* Kiyana said a quick prayer before she picked up the pills. Tears began to fill her eyes as she swallowed them. She knew that God was with her, but she also knew that she still had to fight through it herself. "Good girl, now take your clothes off. You like fucking random niggas, right?" the intruder spoke sarcastically but still calm. "And don't think about those guns either, we found them." Every word he spoke made Kiyana's skin crawl. She stayed quiet as she tried to keep her nerves calm. Another man walked into the room speaking to the man who seemed to be in charge. "I didn't find anything," he had a heavy Jamaican accent and Kiyana noted it in her head. "Okay. Stand watch outside while they clean that mess up," the intruder ordered. He stood up and walked over to Kiyana. He slid his hand down her face and across her lips. Catching her completely off guard he slapped blood in her mouth. "Where's Eve?" he asked again. Leaning over and holding her face, Kiyana spit blood out of her mouth before she spoke. "I told you I don't know," she tried to sound convincing. She looked the man in his eyes, and she felt like she knew him. "Okay," he replied as he slapped her again. Kiyana let out a painful moan this time, but she didn't cry. She kept quiet as he threw her on the bed. Climbing on top of her, he smiled as he leaned over her face touching her nose with his. It was almost as if the intruder had a fetish for Kiyana. He licked her neck with his large wet tongue and Kiyana felt disgusted. Noticing that he placed his gun on the nightstand, she thought about making an attempt to escape. He was still sucking and licking on her neck like he was eating dessert. Kiyana felt even more disgusted.

She closed her eyes and counted to three in her head. On three she kneed the intruder in his balls and elbowed him as hard as she could in his eye. "Fucking bitchh!" He yelled out as he fell off of her. This was the first time he raised his voice since he broke into her home and Kiyana knew he was upset. She had to make it across her king-sized bed to the nightstand. When she was almost there, the intruder grabbed her ankle so hard that Kiyana jerked and hit her head on the tip of the nightstand. Dragging her back across the bed he flipped her over and began to strangle her. Kiyana was half awake half out of it, from the blow to her head and the tight grip around her neck.

Realizing that he wasn't going to let her go, she tried to gain energy. With all of her strength she balled her fists up and swung uncontrollably until he had no choice but to let her neck go. Gasping for air, feeling half dead, Kiyana was relieved that he let his grip go. Grabbing her by her hair now, the intruder raised his fist ready to punch her face in. "ALRIGHT! ALRIGHT! Please, please stop. I won't try to fight you anymore, I swear. Just please don't hit me anymore," Kiyana gave in as she cried out. She was no match for this man, and he had no sympathy for her

being a woman. He would beat her to
death right in her own house if she
made him. "Say please again bitch," the
intruder spoke with anger in his voice.
He kept his fist raised letting her know
that she could still be punched. "Please,
please, pretty please," Kiyana begged.
"Say it one more time," he demanded
as he gripped her hair tighter.
"PLEASEEEEEEE?" Kiyana begged
like a child. The intruder pulled her hair
harder, and she dragged her moan out
longer and louder. He pushed her on
the floor as he got up. "Go take a
shower," he told her as he took his shirt

off. "And hurry up," he spoke firmly. Kiyana got up and did as she was told.

As she stood under the hot water her body began to feel funny. It started with a tingly feeling in her vagina. It felt like she was horny x1000. *"Wow, what the hell did this nigga give me?"* Kiyana thought to herself. The rest of her body began to become tingly and for a second Kiyana couldn't feel herself breath. She grabbed her chest to make sure it was moving as she tried to calm herself down. Tears began to fall from her eyes again and she couldn't control them. She stepped out of the shower leaving the water running and wiped the fog off a spot on the mirror. Looking at herself, she told herself to calm down. "Your just high right now Ki, it's just like poppin a perc and smoking, you've felt this before," Even though she had never felt like this before in her life, Kiyana tried to convince herself otherwise. *"It's obvious that this nigga has a thing for you, you can take advantage of this whole situation,"* she continued to speak to herself silently while staring in the mirror. *"Tune the circumstances you're in out and pretend you're back at work. Give this nigga what he wants and save your life,"* Kiyana finished her thought. She took a deep breath and left the bathroom a changed woman. When she came out of the bathroom, she gasped. The same man who drugged and beat her was butt ass naked with his dick standing tall. There was no way out now, she knew this man was going to rape her. She remembered everything she told herself in the bathroom. She was going to take advantage of the situation. The biggest problem for Kiyana was how huge the rapist's cock was. She had been with a lot of men, but she had never seen anything so huge. "Are you ready to tell me where Eve is?" he asked her. Kiyana was not a snitch. She knew that these men wanted to hurt Eve, so she wasn't gonna give her up. "I don't know where she is. I said that already," she lied. The man smiled. "Okay so I'm going to literally fuck you until you tell me. Get over here and let's see how much dick you can really handle," he yelled. Kiyana took a deep breath and did as she was told. She walked as straight as she could considering her dizziness from the drugs. Her head was spinning a little, but she saw his huge dick clearly and was afraid. *"Just act like he's a customer. Do it like old times,"* a voice said in Kiyana's head. She shed a tear because she knew the less painful way out of this situation was to enjoy the moment. Kiyana screamed out loud startling the intruder. She then dropped down on her knees and crawled to him. She began to give him head. Kiyana's head game was bomb and she loved to give head, it turned her on. She figured she'd take control of her own rape. She thought that sucking his dick would make it easier for her to take it. The intruder was shocked that she was offering head. He wasn't sure if it was a trap, but it felt amazing. He couldn't stop her. She was sucking him off so good that he wanted to eat her out. He had to remember that this was a rape not a date. He let Kiyana suck him off until she tried to stop. "Oh, you don't wanna cum for me big daddy?" Kiyana asked the intruder, completely confusing him. She made him feel like she wanted him. "No, I wanna cum in your pussy and get you pregnant so you won't ever forget me," the intruder said crazily to

Kiyana. She was dealing with a psycho. He motioned for her to get off her knees and she did. He laid her on the bed and slid his dick inside of her. Kiyana screamed out loud. She was trying to enjoy it the best she could, but his cock was huge. After a few strokes, she relaxed and got more into it. She was taking the dick now and moaning. She wanted the rapist to cum as quickly as possible, so she threw her ass back on his dick. She yelled and moaned and made it seem like consensual sex. The intruder's head was fucked up, but he was enjoying it. Kiyana busted nuts on his dick and all. After cumming a few times, she began to wonder when he was going to be finished. She wasn't sure how much longer she could pretend for. An hour had to have passed by, and the intruder was still humping on Kiyana. She couldn't take it anymore, the drugs were helping her enjoy it but she needed a break. "Let me suck on that big cock daddy," Kiyana moaned out, trying to stop him. "Nope, I wanna fuck," he responded. Kiyana closed her eyes and tried her best to stay calm while this man continued to pound on her. She was literally all cummed out and her insides were burning. She closed her eyes and cried as this man had his way with her. Minutes later, Kiyana's house phone rung and the automated caller ID system announced, "Best bitch Eve is calling." The intruder suddenly stopped humping. Kiyana didn't know if it was a good thing that Eve was calling but she was glad that she didn't have any more dick pounding on her. "Answer the phone," the intruder demanded while slowly sliding his dick out of her. Kiyana took a deep breath and did what she was told.

EVE

Eve laid in the same spot for what felt like weeks. She couldn't eat or sleep thinking about Tyrone. *"Why do I love him so much? Why am I like this over him?"* She'd ask herself over and over. She couldn't understand it. Half of her hated him and the other half wanted him right there with her. She didn't know if leaving him hurt more or the fact he was having a baby. She thought about the message that Clarice texted her earlier. She was in labor and soon her soulmate's child with another woman would be born. Eve thought about whether she could ever accept the baby and stay with Tyrone. She imagined Clarice coming to their home to pick her baby up. "No way," she thought in her head. Clarice would have to be out of the picture completely for Eve to accept it. She thought about Tyrone going to her son's school plays and sports events. She couldn't stomach the fact that another woman shared this with him. She shared more with him than Eve with just a baby. Eve took a gulp of her water. Water had become her best-friend since she started her medication for Gono. Her vagina felt disgusting as she thought about what Tyrone gave her. She touched her empty stomach that she thought would never be able to hold babies. *"How the hell didn't I know I had this shit?"* she questioned herself as she cried and wished that she would've known earlier. *"This nigga took life from me,"* Eve thought to herself as she cried more. As she felt the tears rolling down her face, she began to feel stupid. She hated feeling vulnerable and even with just her in the room she felt like someone was watching and laughing at her tears. She wiped her face off and dried her eyes as she took a deep breath. *"Relax E you're good"* she told herself. Grabbing her weed off the dresser she rolled a blunt and smoked as she thought about her next move. She thought about her friend Kiyana, and how she was always down to ride with her and die for her. No matter what was going down, she was ready. Eve's heart began to feel heavy. She knew that with everything she had gone through with Tyrone, her friend was right there and all she ever wanted was the best for her. She picked up the phone to call her. The first time she called her cell it rung once and went to voicemail. The second time she called it did the same. The third time she decided to call her house phone, Kiyana answered on the third ring, "Bitch where you at?" Kiyana asked right away. Eve immediately knew something was wrong. This was their "secret code word" they always had since becoming friends. They knew that one thing that they better not do was to call each other asking 'where you at,' and on top of that, Kiyana knew exactly where she was. "Damn, you all up in my business, hi to you too!" Eve responded trying to stay calm. She could hear the fear in her friend's voice, and she didn't want to alarm whoever was listening, if there was somebody listening. "Nah, because I think somebody might be looking for you or something." Kiyana spoke more in code, and Eve was thankful that they had created it but hated to use it. "Girl ain't nobody looking for me but my nigga Tyrone." Eve played the laugh off and continued to speak, "and I spoke to him, he's coming to get me."

Eve hoped like hell that she was helping Kiyana's situation. "I knew you were with his ass. Ok girl, call me later," Kiyana said and then hung up the phone. Eve had no idea what to do or what the fuck kind of trouble her friend was in. She got down on her knees and prayed for her best friend. Something said to call her, and to now know that she was in trouble was nerve wrecking. She stayed on her knees and prayed for hours…

CLUE LANCE & KIYANA.

Lance was driving with no destination, still trying to get in contact with Eve with no success. He knew that Kiyana told him she was alright, but he wanted to hear from her himself. He was fed up with the secrets and he wanted to speak to her. Kiyana was the only one who seemed to be able to talk to her and she owed him pussy anyway, so he decided to drive to her house. Clue got caught up with some business shit the night he was supposed to see Kiyana and he had to get rid of all of his phones. He had a serious situation going on. Things had died down a little now, so he decided to go finish what he had left off. He knew Kiyana and knew that she would accept his apology better in person than she would over the phone. He didn't bother to call her. He jumped in his car and headed over to her house. Lance pulled up on Kiyana's block and he decided to drive past before just showing up. When he did, he noticed that her door had been kicked in. He immediately thought that something was wrong. He kept driving and parked around the corner. He had his nine-millimeter on him, he was one who never left home without a strap.

Instead of going right in, he snuck in quietly. He wasn't sure what he was going to be walking in on. Lance slid into the doorway quietly. He heard talking coming from Kiyana's room. He creeped through the house slowly and the closer he got to her room the clearer he could hear the talking. Kiyana was on the phone with Eve. He hid in the hallway and listened to Eve tell Kiyana that she was about to meet up with her man. Lance felt stupid for a second. Here he was creeping in this girl's house, and she was fine, chatting with Eve. He was worried sick about

Eve, and she sound perfectly fine on the phone. Before he decided to creep back out of the house, he heard a man's voice. "You lucky bitch. you've been touched by an angel," the man's voice said. Lance wasn't sure if he should think anything of it. He was feeling like a creep being in her house, but her door was kicked in. Before he could turn around and leave, he heard someone pulling up outside. Initially he was going to exit through the front door but now he was heading back inside. Suddenly, he heard Kiyana screaming. "No, get the fuck off of me now. You got what you wanted." Kiyana was screaming and it was obvious that she needed help. Before Lance could do anything, a man came running through and kicked in Kiyana's room door. He was firing off shots right away. It was Clue. When he had pulled up to Kiyana's place, her front door was kicked off the hinges. He wasted no time coming in to see what was going on. He heard Kiyana screaming and lost it. He shot the naked man that was on top of her first. And then another one came out of the closet. Two more men came running into the room surprising Lance. He didn't see where they came from. Just that quick, Lance was in a shootout. He saw that Clue was helping Kiyana so he was automatically on his side. He came through the door and opened fire on the last two men standing, killing them instantly. He saw a naked man lying dead and Clue holding Kiyana's naked body. He assumed that this was one of her niggas and he felt awkward. Clue looked at Kiyana's face with disgust. Her lips were swollen, and her eyes were black and blue swollen. He grabbed one of her robes out of her closet and threw it around her. He picked her up and began to carry her outside to his car, he stopped to talk to the man that just helped save his life. "I'm Clue, I'm getting her out of here. You can follow us to my house if you need her," Clue told him. "I'm Lance, I'm Eve's cousin. I'm looking for Eve. I'll follow you." He responded. Clue, Lance and Kiyana left the house, Kiyana sat in the passenger seat of Clue's car, grateful that he had saved her. She was able to breathe easy now, but the drugs were still taking a toll on her. She was tired. She drifted off to sleep, feeling safe in Clue's hands. When they reached Clue's house he carried her inside, still sleeping. He was so sorry that this happened to her. He loved Kiyana. He laid her on his bed and went to run her a bath. He made her some tea and woke her up when it was finished. "Get into the hot bath and drink this tea," he told her. Kiyana didn't refuse a thing. Her heart was melting over how sweet Clue was treating her. His soft side for her was real. Kiyana sat in the bath and sipped her tea as she began to process what had just happened to her. Clue and

Lance sat in the living room together, confused. They had both walked into some shit they had to turn into a horror scene. It was their first-time meeting, and they were killing people together. "Yo, thank you for having my back earlier. I don't even know you, but you came through," Clue told Lance. "I was there to help Kiyana and so were you, so we had the same opps," Lance responded. Suddenly, his phone rung. Finally, it was Eve. He answered quickly.

"Yo Eve, what the fuck is going on? Where are you?" Lance asked her immediately. "Listen Lance, I can't talk to you about that right now, I need you to go check on Kiyana for me," she insisted, sounding scared. "She's good. Me and a friend of mine got her. Now you got some explaining to do, or I ain't telling you shit else," he demanded. Eve took a deep breath; she was so pleased to hear that her friend was safe. She wondered how Lance saved her, but she knew he wasn't going to give her any more information. She had to spill the beans. She couldn't hold in what Tyrone did to her anymore. She was embarrassed but she had to tell. She cried as she told Lance the truth from the beginning to the end. Lance listened and anger built up inside of him. He didn't like how hurt Eve was. After finishing his phone convo with Eve, he told Clue everything. They concluded that they both had to find Tyrone. Clue thought hard about who could help find him. He was in The DR but he wasn't untouchable. Suddenly, he knew just who to call. He excused himself from the living room and went outside to make his call. He was going to find Tyrone and he was going to make him pay for what he had done to Kiyana and Eve.

TOMMI

Tommi smiled at the notification she received; it was another $1500 from Tyrone. In total he had sent $3000 for Tommi to make a phone call. Tommi was an investor. She made money and let her money make her more money. She was into everything. She was a single mother, and she busted her ass for her children. She owned businesses and had connections. She had dibble dabbled in illegal activities in her past but she was legit now. But she never lost her hustle. Tyrone asked her to investigate Eve's case with the doctor's office, this was the easiest money she had ever made. Shortly after handling Tyrone's job, Tommi received another phone call. This phone call put all the pieces together. *If only Tyrone knew*, she thought.

TYRONE

Tyrone arrived overseas just in time for the birth of his first child and son. Clarice was so happy that her son waited for his father's arrival. She was crowning when he walked into the room. She was beyond emotional and although her mother and grandmother were there with her every step of the way, she was yearning for her man. Tyrone jumped right into action. He was holding Clarice's hand and rubbing her head with a towel when her final push brought life into the world. Tyrone heard his son's cries and his heart melted. At that very moment, nothing in the world mattered to him, not Eve not Kiyana, and not even Lance, nothing but his child. Grandma Nelli laid their big, beautiful baby boy on Clarice's chest and Tyrone watched the mother of his child cry happy tears. He watched how she gazed at him in amazement. They had created something special together for the first time. They had created a life that either of them would die for. Tyrone's heart was filled with a newfound love. Together they named their son Tyrone Jr., he was 10 pounds even. Hours went by as they bonded as a family and

Clarice finally allowed herself to sleep. Of course, Tyrone Jr. had to sleep right next to her. Tyrone was watching them sleep. He was standing there in awe when Clarice's grandmother requested to speak with him privately. "Follow me," she requested as she walked down a long hallway. She stopped in front of a black door and turned to him. "Welcome to the family Tyrone, The Family would like to speak with you," she spoke in her heavy accent as she turned back around and entered the room. When they entered, all the chatter that was going on inside the room stopped. It was silent. Tyrone was more curious than nervous. He had never been in this room before, but he always listened to the stories that Clarice would tell him about what went down in it. Although he did business with the men in her family, he had never met them personally. He always had to meet a 'middleman,' so he had never met or dealt with them directly. He was pleased that they were finally going to meet. He knew having a son with Clarice, meant he was officially drawn in for life. The room had black and white checkered walls. The pattern would make you dizzy if you looked too long, but it was exquisite. The carpet was the colors of the Dominican flag, and it was beautiful. It was full fluffy and looked like it would massage your toes if you walked on it barefoot. There was a beautiful chandelier shaped like the letter P, it was something that Tyrone had never seen. Every piece of furniture looked custom and expensive, like the décor found in homes in the magazines. After admiring every detail, he laid his eyes on the corner of the room. There was a red pool table where two men and one lady were seated. Tyrone assumed that they must have been family members of Clarice…the one's she'd always spoke of. He expected a bigger family. The pool table was set up for a game of pool, but it was almost too hard to tell if that's what it was used for. It was set so nicely that it looked as if it had never been touched. The balls were shinning, and the sticks were sharp. The men sitting at the table sat with confidence, their faces were not friendly at all. The lady was breathtakingly beautiful and smiling. She spoke to Tyrone first, "Welcome to the family, Tyrone." She had the most beautiful voice he had ever heard. Her heavy accent made it even sexier. Tyrone was almost mesmerized. Before he could swallow his spit to speak, she continued talking as if she was never waiting for him to respond. "Congratulations on your first child and your first son. Welcome to the hood of eternity. It's almost a blessing to have that combination, and I say almost because all children are blessings. So, I believe it is even more of a blessing or a privilege to have that combination. As I welcome you into the family, I would like to inform you of the importance of your responsibility. Our men matter. Our women are special. We take family very seriously. I am certain that you will be a great father. So, I speak on behalf of the entire family when I say we would like to gift you," the lady spoke. She then reached her right hand out towards the man to the right of her. "Pretty Ricky," the man said with a straight face and stern voice. She then reached her left hand out and did the same with the man to the left. "Paulie," the man to the left spoke easier than the first man.

"Patricia," the lady than said, placing her two right fingers over her lips then putting it down. "We would like to gift you your life. You see, the family and I are very aware of your dealings back in the states," Patricia paused. Tyrone had no idea what was going on or what the hell they were talking about. "I don…" Tyrone began to speak and before he could finish his second word a dart flew across the room hitting the wall, just missing his face. "Don't speak," the beautiful soft voice that first had him mesmerized was now vicious and evil. Tyrone swallowed hard this time, afraid. He kept his mouth shut. "Now, what do you have to say for yourself?" Patricia asked. Tyrone kept quiet and then another dart flew past even closer than the first. "Speak," Patricia demanded. Tyrone was livid, but he held it in. For some reason, unlike any other time, he did not want to die for his pride. He stayed calm and hoped to make it out alive. "I'm not sure what dealings you're speaking of. I only do business dealings and you all are my only business partners," Tyrone answered honestly to his best ability. "Enough of the bullshit. We're speaking of your dealings with Eve Passion. We know all about it. We do not allow disrespect or disloyalty to our women. As I said before, we are special. Now that you have a brand-new responsibility with our lady, Clarice, we can't just kill you off. Therefore, we are gifting you your life, HERE only. If you do not agree you can be arranged to be put at peace tonight. If you're the man that Clarice believed you to be, you will walk away from that life back home right now. So, Tyrone, what is your decision?" Patricia asked. Tyrone was completely shocked. He thought that he had kept his life back home separated from his life in DR. He felt every word that Patricia said in his soul. It was not just life or death to him, it meant leaving Eve. Leaving their unborn. If there was one. Leaving their whole life together. He still had no idea what was going on back home. What kind of man would he be if he just vanished, he thought? But what kind of man would he be if he didn't think about the most important person in his life now, his son. His child with Clarice was here, Eves wasn't. It would be selfish of him to put anyone's happiness before his son's, including his own. "Can I think about it?" Tyrone asked sincerely. He was in a state of shock with this decision. "Sure" Patricia smiled as she answered. "We already prepared to give you 10 minutes. You have seven left." She told him. The Family wasn't playing any games with Tyrone. They meant everything they told him. Tyrone swallowed hard. He was sweating while thinking. Suddenly his phone vibrated. It was a message from an unknown number. *Eve isn't pregnant, the job is done.* The message broke his heart and he tried to keep his composure. For a second Tyrone thought about running and leaving the room. But reality crept right in, he remembered he had about 5 more minutes now to choose. Replaying the message in his head he was so confused. It killed him not to know what was going on with Eve. Although now she made it easier for him to decide between his kids. He had no choice but to leave everything he knew back home, back home. He swallowed his pride and lived for his son. "I choose life here," Tyrone replied.

"Well done," Patricia stated. "We'll take care of everything back home for you, don't worry about a thing. Do not reach out to no one. We will give you a new cellular device. Today begins your new life with your new family. Welcome to The Family."

ONE WEEK LATER

TOMMI

Tommi's doorbell rung, and she knew who it was. She was expecting company tonight and she was overdue for what they were bringing…head. Clue had been eating Tommi's pums for years now without ever fucking. No one knew but them. Tommi loved keeping her business on the low anyway, and Clue didn't want to look like a sucker. He just couldn't help it, Tommi's pussy taste so good. And she was great to have on your team. She opened the door and let him in. "Hey babe, what's up? Come in," she said as she greeted him at the door. Clue walked in and right over to the couch, making himself at home. "I don't have much time tonight," he told her. "Im still staying low from that shit that just went down. And thanks for cleaning that mess up. I need to know what's up with old boy Tyrone. Why haven't you gotten back to me about him yet?" Clue sounded frustrated. Tommi stayed calm. "Clue…baby, I'm doing my best to find him. Don't worry," she lied. "Yeah, aight Tommi. Just bring that pussy over here. I gotta go," he demanded. Tommi smiled. She loved the way Clue ate her pussy; he was her favorite eater of them all. She felt bad for lying to him, she knew he wanted to hurt Tyrone. The truth of the matter was, when Clue called Tommi and told her everything about Tyrone, Tommi knew exactly who and where he was. Tommi had connections all over, and people underestimated her sometimes. She knew Clarice, she knew her family, she knew it all. She did everybody a favor by personally telling "The Family" everything that Tyrone had done. She knew they didn't play about their women and that they would take care of Tyrone. Tommi swore not to tell. She hated lying to Clue but her name was on the line. She couldn't ruin that. She put her focus back on receiving head.

To Be Continued…

CARMEN & HAZE

Carmen admired her naked body in her ceiling mirror as she exhaled the blunt of Kush from her lungs. The silk sheets touching her skin and spreading across her king-sized bed was doing something to her. She was extremely horny, and lonely. Her bent legs were moving back and forth and the feeling of her vagina lips opening, and closing was moistening up her pussy. She watched her pink fingernails rub across her titties, as her nipples hardened. She teased the tip of her nipples before sliding her fingers down across her stomach to the top of her vagina. She slid her middle finger slowly up and down her clit. She closed her eyes as she imagined having the touch of a man grabbing and squeezing her thighs and butt cheeks. Her imagination sent a warm sensation through her private parts. She rubbed her clit as she continued to imagine this man touching on her and then she imagined another man joining. One of Carmen's secret fantasies was getting gang banged. She closed her eyes and continued to rub on her pussy as she imagined every hole on her body being occupied with dick. She fantasized and rubbed on herself until she climaxed. After finishing she felt better, but she knew it would be a matter of time before she was horny again. Carmen had a fucking problem...literally. She loved to fuck, and she was addicted to having orgasms. It was so bad that Carmen was on her way to a sex addict meeting. She had no idea what else would help her. She was tired of pleasing herself. She realized that having one-night stands put her into scary situations, and she was lonely. Her addiction to sex kept her from keeping a man. Her last option was to see if maybe it was a mental thing and whether or not she could help it. She took a cold shower and headed out for the meeting.

Carmen laughed at herself sitting in a meeting with a bunch of sex addicts. She couldn't believe this is what her life had come down to. Did she really need a professional to tell her what her problem was? She liked to fuck, and she didn't see any issues with that. Maybe the people, places, and things that she chose to fuck could've been a little concerning, but she was sure that there were worse stories than hers. And here she was sitting with a bunch of sex addicts, about to find out.

As everyone greeted each other and found their seats, she noticed a fine ass man had entered the room. He was absolutely stunning to Carmen. He was dark skinned, tatted-up, and his dreads were healthy and long. She fixed herself and sat up in her seat as she felt her vagina begin to cream. This man was turning her on in the worse way and she was almost embarrassed. Here she was at a sex addict meeting and one of the members had her ready to fuck right in the middle of the floor, in front of everybody. She took a deep breath and relaxed herself. She didn't want the extreme horniness she was feeling to be obvious in a room full of sex addicts. The mystery man sat down as if he was in a familiar place. The room continued to fill up with people, but Carmen couldn't take her eyes or mind off her newest victim. She told herself that she was gonna have him before the night was over.

"Good evening, everyone. Welcome to Can't Stop Fucking Sex Addicts Anonymous," the instructor

spoke as she walked into the room.
"CSFSAA for short," she said. It grew
quiet as if being quiet when she spoke
was a rule that everyone knew. The
instructor was absolutely beautiful.
She looked like she was straight from
an island. Her smooth brown skin
was beautiful, and it had a shine to it.
Her natural hair was cut short. It fit
her face perfectly. Although it was
cut, her hair was thick and very
healthy. Her eyes were a deep green,
and they were mesmerizing. Carmen
caught herself starring hard at the

instructor. This woman had more of an effect on her than the chocolate dread head did. Now she was having thoughts of all three of them fucking. In her head she imagined the dread head fucking the instructor while she played with her pussy at the same time. Carmen thought about the way she would look at the dread head while waiting for her turn to be pounded on. She imagined the instructor moaning while she rubbed on her clit. She pictured herself putting her tittie in the instructor's mouth and her sucking on it. She pictured the dread head throwing the instructor to the side, slapping her ass, and motioning for Carmen to come to him. She pictured herself crawling to the dread head on all fours. After crawling over to him, she turns around and lifts her leg across his stomach getting into doggy style position. She rubs her pussy up and down on his cock until it slips inside of her. She imagined herself gasping due to the dread heads cock being so huge. She imagined bouncing slowly up and down on him while the instructor spread her legs open putting her pussy in Carmen's face. Carmen imagines eating the instructors bare beautiful coochie. Before Carmen knew it, she was grinding on her chair in the middle of the meeting. She had to catch herself and come back to her senses. She looked around to see if anyone noticed but everyone seemed to be paying attention to the person speaking. Carmen was so caught up in her dirty thoughts she didn't realize that the session had begun. A few people later, it was Carmen's turn to introduce herself. "Hello, my name is Carmen. I'm 25 years old and I'm a sex addict. I've been having sex since I was 17," she answered what was asked. She wasn't volunteering any extra information like the others. It was bad enough that she was there, she thought. Carmen listened until it was time for dread head to speak. "My name is Haze, I'm 29, and I'm a sex addict," was all he said, and Carmen was head over hills already. Just from hearing his voice alone. It was sexy to her. She couldn't help but imagine him asking her "*who's pussy is this*" She was turned on bad. Of course, after the dread head it was the instructors turn. "My name is Jazmiine and I'm 44 years old. I'm a sex addict and I've been sexually active since I was 14," she said. Carmen thought the name Jazmiine fit her well. It seemed exotic.

The group meeting continued, and Carmen stayed quiet. It wasn't mandatory for her to engage so she just listened. Marriages and families were being ruined because of people's addictions to sex. Carmen thought if she was ever married, she would never cheat, but she couldn't even stay faithful in a relationship now. She was addicted to dick, and she always ended up cheating.

The meeting was over now, and Carmen was watching Haze's movements like a hawk. She waited until he was by himself to approach him. "What's up?" Carmen asked in her sweet seductive voice. "Aint shit, wad up?" Haze answered with the same voice that turned her on earlier. "Ima keeps it real with you. I want you to fuck the shit out of me," Carmen was completely honest with Haze. He was either gonna take it or leave it. Haze laughed. "Oh yeah?" he asked. "So, it's like that huh?" he continued. "Yes please," Carmen begged a little. "It's been a while," she added in. Haze laughed harder. "Yeah, and I'm a virgin," he mocked, expressing his disbelief. "Listen, I'm grown, it's been a minute, and I want you. So, is we fucking or what?"

Carmen was straight up with Haze and wanted an answer. Haze looked her up and down before responding. "We out," he responded before leading the way. Carmen followed Haze, smiling from ear to ear while her pussy was throbbing.

"So, is this something you always do?" Haze asked Carmen while driving home. "I mean it's been a while," Carmen replied. "It's been a while since you did this? Or do you mean it's been a while since you've been fucked on?" Haze asked her.

"Both," Carmen replied while starring at him. Hearing him say *"fucked on"* turned her on. She couldn't control her hormones around Haze. She wasn't sure if he was special or if she was just super horny because it had been so long. Either way she was going to find out. "How long 'til we get to your house cause I'm ready to fuck right now," she told him. "Right now, right now?" Haze asked, smiling, and joking. Her sexy, horny self was amusing to him. Carmen watched him smirk and imagined his juicy lips sucking on her clit. She honestly couldn't wait to get to their destination. She would've given him head while he was driving but she just met him and she knew that once she started, she wouldn't be able to stop. She wanted to get fucked in a bed. She wondered how deep the sex could get being that they were both addicts. Haze didn't seem like an addict to Carmen, but she figured he was just holding back for now. She couldn't wait to see what he was like in bed.

Finally, they arrived at his house and went straight to his bedroom. Carmen couldn't control herself any longer. She was literally all over Haze. She took charge, pulled his shirt off and was licking all over his chest. Haze allowed her to do what she wanted. He laughed at how wild this stranger was getting with him. Carmen had his pants down now and was admiring his penis. It was just as big as she had imagined. She wanted to be fucked but she was not going to suck his dick. One thing she kept to herself in her nasty world was her mouth. She decided when, where, and how she would use it. Tonight, wasn't the night. Haze was too fine to her; she couldn't give it all up to him right away. She thought, after rubbing his dick with her soft hands. She then stood up and took her shirt off. She unfastened her bra and threw it across the room. She massaged her own breast while locking eyes with Haze. He stood there naked and beautiful to her. "You wanna touch on me?"

Carmen asked Haze in her seductive voice.

"No, I wanna fuck on you," Haze responded. Carmen moaned "Hmm I want you to fuck me all night," she replied. Her hand was now rubbing on her pussy. She kept her eyes locked on Haze's eyes. He was biting his lip. He grabbed her by her ass cheeks and lifted her off the floor. Carmen wrapped her legs around him as he walked her into a wall. Pinned up, she kissed Haze like it was their wedding day. "Just fuck me please," Carmen moaned and begged. Haze carried her back across the room and threw her on the bed. Carmen rolled over onto her stomach and sat up on all fours. Sitting doggy style, she rocked up and down while shaking her ass, making it clap. She was horny and ready to be pleased. Haze slid behind her and tapped on her ass with his penis. "You ready for me?" he asked seductively. "I've been ready since you walked into the 'can't stop fucking' sex meeting," she said. Haze laughed. "Yeah, I saw you day-dreaming about the kid." He joked. "What were you thinking about?" he asked her.

"This exact moment right here," she replied. Carmen was telling the truth without adding the extra details about the instructor. "You pounding my shit out doggy style," Carmen finished. Haze was mesmerized. Everything about Carmen was making his dick hard but he couldn't help but think that she was this way with everybody. They were complete strangers, and he had her ass naked on his bed, on her knees, begging for dick. Her being a sex addict didn't make it any better. Haze shook these thoughts out of his head and enjoyed the moment. If it wasn't his pussy, it was at least his for the night. He was gonna do what he wanted with it. He slid his dick inside of her slowly at first and Carmen gasped. Her pussy was so tight and moist Haze could feel it beating on his dick. He stroked her slow as she gyrated on him. He was making love to her from the back. He fucked Carmen for hours and she fucked him back. She made him tap out. When they finished, he couldn't get out of his head. He wanted to lock Carmen in his room forever. He was hooked and he didn't want nobody else having her. He knew he should have known better than this, but he couldn't help it. He was going to turn a whore into a housewife.

The next day Carmen woke up in love. She didn't wanna leave Haze and go home alone. She wanted to move in with him. She knew she couldn't ask him about these crazy thoughts, but she wanted what she wanted. She'd been nothing but real with Haze since she met him, so she figured she'd keep it that way. "Haze wake up," she shook him slightly until he woke up. "What's up babe? What's wrong?" Haze asked a little annoyed at her for waking him out of his sleep. "We need to talk. Sit up," she requested in a serious voice. "Man, I know this ain't no Dashiki shit, don't tell me you pregnant already," Haze joked. He had a great sense of humor. Carmen laughed with him. "Haze, I wanna be with you. I know this is sudden and fast, and we just met yesterday but I know what I want when I want it. I want you," Carmen blurted out her confession. Haze was in awe inside. He already wanted her just as bad and now he didn't have to do much work. She wanted the same thing. "I love you too babe. We go together now," Haze told her as he laughed. "I'm serious," Carmen laughed. "We're sex addicts and I know it's gonna be hard, but I know exactly what we can do to make it work. We're gonna make a sex

435

calendar for the new year. So, we can finish December off just going with the flow," Carmen told him. Haze had no idea what a sex calendar was, and he was in no mood to ask. He was still tired, and it sounded freaky, so he just agreed. "Okay babe. Now let's lay back down," he told her and cuddled her back to sleep.

Days turned into weeks, and they were inseparable. The new year was upon them. Carmen and Haze came up with a sex calendar for the first six months of the year. They

436

figured that this would be the perfect way to satisfy their addiction while staying faithful. If they both agreed to their terms and conditions, nothing else mattered.

JANUARY

January was going to be "**Just us January**." They would start the year off with being exclusive, having sex with each other only. They thought this way they would know they still had real love for each other. They would succumb to their addiction for 31 days. During January it would be all about them and only them.

January was a beautiful breeze. It was easy for them to fiend for each other because it was just the beginning. They both knew this, but they felt like they were soul mates. They went on a date every Friday and Saturday of the month. They tried all kinds of dates from restaurants to movies, to roller skating and picnics at the park. They dated and did everything together. They were inseparable. On Sundays they stayed in, watching their favorite movies and shows. On Tuesdays they told each other about a secret from their addiction. They bonded very well during the month of January and Carmen was proud of herself. Although they were only two months in, she didn't even have thoughts of cheating like she had in her past.

All she cared about was Haze. Their dates were like being out with a best friend plus some extra loving. Each date ended with them humping in random ass places. It was always a spur of the moment type thing. They turned each other on so much. Haze couldn't make it through a movie date without rubbing on Carmen's clit. Every date was not only fun as fuck, but it was also sexual. It was just what they both needed. Their picnic date ended with orgasms during the sunset. That was one of Carmen's favorite dates. They were in pure bliss. *"Carmen and Haze"* was all Carmen breathed. She was sprung.

FEBRUARY

After January things heated up. February was **"Fuck Fest Friday February."** This month actually excited Carmen. She was a secret member of "Pretty's Box." "Pretty's Box" was a secret location where there were secret events and secret fantasies taken place. To sum it up, it was a mansion party of sexual activities. Some members were single, and some were married. But all members were with whatever went down at PB's. Anything sexual you could think of went on. Carmen was a regular and the orgy rooms at Pretty's Box were her favorite. So, to have her own fuck fest at home with her man was making her vagina's heart beat. The rules were, they would start the month off slow, they would each invite only one other person of their liking to join them while fucking. Carmen and Haze were allowed to give each other one rule to abide by while choosing their other person. Haze's rule for Carmen was no men as her plus one; and Carmen's rule for Haze was no ex's that he spent more than 6 months with. They both agreed to their rules and had no issues. Their first fuck fest would be the first Friday of the month. The outcome of their first one would determine the rest of their Fridays.

Carmen wanted to host the first event at her house, she was well equipped for the occasion. Her room had a screw in stripper pole that she had recently took down while on her "no dick binge." She was more than ecstatic to be putting it back up. Haze saw the sparkle in Carmen's eyes as she prepared for the event. He was dealing with a true freak. She had handcuffs, whips, chains, vibrators...all kinds of things. She had so much sex shit that Haze became a little nervous. He couldn't lie though, he loved all of it.

It was Friday morning, and they were both anxious about their upcoming event. Carmen was a little curious about who Haze was bringing but she trusted that he would follow the rules. Haze was like a kid going to the candy store. He was overly excited. He honestly didn't care who Carmen brought as long as there were no niggas. He felt like the man himself, knowing he was going to be pleased by three freaks tonight. There was no way they weren't freaks, considering that they were agreeing to some shit like this, he thought.

It was 6:00 PM and it was showtime. Carmen dressed in a black lingerie set and black silk robe. Haze had on matching black silk boxers. The stripper pole was up and all of Carmen's sex gadgets were spread across the couch in her room. The doorbell rang and they both smiled at each other. One, if not both, of their victims had arrived. Haze's bitch arrived first. Carmen was amazed but pleased to see such a fine ass woman showing up to fuck her man. She looked her up and down. She was close to perfect. She was dark chocolate with white pretty teeth. When she smiled she looked like a baby. Carmen wondered how long Haze was with this gorgeous barbie. She thought there could have been no way that he was with her for less than six months. Her beautiful face alone could melt hearts and on top of that, she was a freak. She had to be for her to show up for the event. Carmen glanced at Haze, wondering if she could really trust him to stick to the rules.

"Hello, I'm Carmen. What's your name?" Carmen greeted her after sizing her up with her eyes.

"Hey Carmen. I'm Caramel. It's nice to meet you as well," Hazes choice spoke in a friendly but sarcastic manner.

"Well, come on in Caramel. Follow me," Carmen walked Caramel into the living room. Here they would sip on some wine and get to know each other a little until their last member showed up.

"So, how long have you known Haze?" Carmen couldn't wait to ask Caramel.

"Well, I've known him for a while, he was a regular at my club at one point in time," she replied. "We were never sexually involved," Caramel added in.

"Oh ok. So, this would be the first time. How interesting," Carmen replied. She wasn't sure how to feel about that. The fact that Haze had never slept with Caramel made Carmen feel like it must have been a fantasy of his. She was far from insecure, but she assumed that he would have picked a bitch that he had already fucked. What if he fell in love with this new pussy? She pushed the thoughts out of her head as quickly as they came. She was secure.

"So, when you say club, do you mean you used to dance?" Carmen continued to find out more about her man's choice.

"Yes, I was a dancer," Caramel answered proudly. Carmen was pleased. She imagined Caramel swinging her chocolate ass all around on her pole. She was going to have a good time with her, she thought.

The doorbell rang again, and this time Haze answered it. He was beyond shocked to see the instructor from the sex addiction group standing on the other side of the door. *My bitch is a bad bitch,* Haze thought to himself as he smiled. The instructor was just as shocked to see Haze. She didn't expect to see any of her group members besides Carmen. She was a little embarrassed, but it was too late now.

"Well, hello instructor," Haze greeted her while licking his lips.

"Please, call me Jazmiine. And have some respect for your elders.

Close your mouth," Jazmiine was feisty outside of her meetings.

Haze was completely turned on. He couldn't believe he would be fucking such a fine ass cougar. He smiled again at the thought of Carmen bagging the instructor for their fuck fest. Everything about Carmen was turning him on. He was ready for a wild crazy night.

"Follow me Jazmiine," he spoke seductively while leading her into the living room. Carmen smiled as

Jazmiine entered, she thought about the first time she saw the instructor and the fantasies that she had at the time. Now she was going to bring them to life. The same way that she did with Haze.

"Well, since everyone is here, I guess we could get started," Carmen spoke. "First, I would like to thank both of you beautiful ladies for being down with this. I wanna say that Haze and I are very much so happy together, but we wanna spice our sex life up. I need both of you beautiful women to know that this is a one-time fuck. None of us will be seeing each other outside of tonight, unless it's under these same circumstances," Carmen spoke firm and loud. "I want tonight to be an amazing experience for all of us. I'm not sure if either of you ladies has done this before, but this is a judge free zone. Anything freaky goes. If at any moment anyone is uncomfortable, please let me know right away. I want tonight to stay exclusively between us. And I don't know, depending how tonight goes, we may be fucking every Friday for the rest of this month," Carmen bussed out laughing after speaking. She wanted to get her speech out of the way so they could get down to business.

"If anyone needs liquor, drugs or anything else to help enhance their time tonight, let me know," she finished up. She gestured for everyone to follow her into her bedroom. And it was showtime.

Carmen had some drinks already poured and sitting out on the dresser. She had blunts rolled and even some e-pills per Haze's request. She flipped her light switch to turn on her red lightbulbs and took her robe off. Her thong lingerie set fit her curvy body in such a sexy way. Her booty jiggled while she strutted across the room to put the radio on. She played soft R & B to get everyone in the mood. It was going to be a long night. Haze watched Carmen move how she moved. She was introducing him to a whole new world, and she was the boss in it. He loved it. It was like the matrix to him. His dick was extremely hard from being in the room with three gorgeous women who were all his for the night. He'd had threesomes before, but the circumstances of this situation made it wilder. He took an e-pill from the dresser and threw it back with a shot of liquor. He watched Caramel take her clothes off and strip down to her bra and panties. They were red lace and glowing on her chocolate skin. He thought about the nights when he used to throw all his money at Caramel when she was stripping at the club. He loved the way she would shake her ass and bust her coochie open. He always wanted to fuck her brains out, but he wasn't one to pay for pussy. At the time, Caramel was for sale only. Now she was free and his for the night. He was going to fuck her good. He wanted to lick Carmen's vagina for having the stripper pole, it made having Caramel even better for him. Carmen watched

Haze watch Caramel. She wasn't going to get in her feelings about it and ruin the night, but she was definitely making a mental note of it. Caramel was fine as fuck, Carmen couldn't front. As soon as Caramel finished taking her clothes off, she hopped her ass right to the pole. She was sexy as shit swinging around it. Watching her dance, Carmen started to understand Haze's fantasy, she couldn't even be mad at his ass.

Jazmiine was throwing shots back like they were juice. Carmen smiled, she wanted her to get highly intoxicated. She couldn't wait to put her hands and mouth on her. Over two months ago she had seen her for the first time and had literally dreamed about being in bed with her. Now here she was, in bed with her, her dreams had come true...right down to Haze being in bed with them. Carmen was amazed and proud of herself. She knew she was a bad bitch and she patted herself on the back for it. She lit her blunt and smiled. "So, who wants to get spanked first?" Haze asked, starting the party up. He picked up Carmen's black whip and swung it in the air. "Me daddy," Caramel replied first. She was still swinging on the pole. Carmen smiled, she liked Caramel's dominance, but Carmen called the shots. Walking over to Haze, Carmen sweetly took the whip from Haze's hand while tongue kissing him and rubbing on his rock-hard penis. "I actually give the spankings out first. I'm in charge for the first hour then it's your turn. Ok daddy?" Carmen asked her man seductively. Almost like role playing. Haze let Carmen do what she does. "Ok, spank some ass babe," he told her. Carmen walked over to Caramel and started rubbing her butt. It was soft. She rubbed it and then began gripping it. Each time she gripped her ass cheek she would pull her vagina lips open with the grip. This was making Caramel wetter than she already was. "So, you want a spanking first huh?" Carmen asked Caramel. "Yes," Caramel answered in a baby voice. Carmen slid her finger across Caramel's clit over her panties very lightly. Her red laced panties were soaked. "Why is your pussy so wet?" Carmen asked her. "I don't know daddy," she replied. "Okay, so Ima spank you for having a wet pussy," Carmen told her while she continued to slightly rub on her clit. "Bend over and touch your toes," Carmen told her. Caramel did what she was told. Her ass was up in the air and spread out. Carmen gently spanked her ass with the whip. Caramel let out a loud moan. Carmen spanked her again harder this time, and Caramel moaned even louder. Haze watched as Carmen spanked his bitch and he loved it. He was ready to give everybody some dick. It was Carmen's hour to be in control, but he couldn't wait any longer. "Come here Carmen," he told her sternly interrupting her spanking session. "Yes Haze," she answered softly, obeying her man, and walking over to him. "I wanna fuck," he demanded. "And I wanna fuck you first," he added. Carmen smiled, she was pleased to know that her man was horny and wanted her, but she was in charge right now...and the rules were the rules. "I know you wanna fuck the shit out of all of us babe but you and big poppa down there gotta wait," she spoke, referring to his large penis, she rubbed his dick through his boxers. "I promise it'll be worth the wait," she added before kissing him. "Lay back and enjoy the show for now," she told him. He did what he was told. He was done trying to bend the rules. Carmen was the boss. Caramel was still listening. She was still bent over touching her toes and shaking her ass. Carmen smiled at Jazmiine watching Caramel shake her ass. "You like what you see?" Carmen asked Jazmiine, interrupting her stare. "As a matter of fact, I do. I love everything I'm seeing right now," Jazmiine flirted back boldly. "Oh yeah? And how much do you love it?" Carmen asked her flirting back just as bold. The instructor walked up to Carmen and began kissing her. Carmen didn't stop her; she kissed her ass right back. The instructor's lips were soft, and her tongue was warm. Her kisses felt good. "Is my spanking over?" Caramel asked interrupting Carmen and Jazmiine. "Nope," Carmen replied as she stopped kissing Jazmiine and went back to Caramel. She spanked her about ten more times, causing her to scream out before she was done. "Now it is," she smiled. Caramel stood up and walked over to Carmen. She was so turned on by her she almost forgot that Haze was there. She kissed Carmen with so much passion. "I wonder how good you can kiss punanie," Carmen said. "Let me show you," Caramel responded. Carmen was in charge, but Caramel was now leading the way. She walked Carmen to her own bed and laid her down on it. Haze had the perfect view. "Spread your legs open," Caramel told Carmen. She listened and obeyed. She spread her legs open as wide as she could. Caramel sat between Carmen's legs admiring her vagina before just jumping in it. She slid her thong off to get a better view. Carmen's vagina was pretty as hell and the butterfly wings she had tatted on it made it so much more appealing. Caramel looked Carmen in the eyes and smiled before she went down on her. She kept eye contact as she licked. Kissed. And sucked on her clit. Carmen didn't moan but she bit her lip uncontrollably and made sexual faces. Caramel wanted her to moan. She sucked harder on her vagina until moans finally crept out of her. Carmen was moaning. She couldn't hold it back anymore. Caramel was giving her some of the best head she had ever had. As Carmen moaned Jazmiine couldn't mind her business any longer. The liquor had long ago kicked in and it was making her hot and horny. She was feeling amazing. She squeezed Carmen's pierced titties as Caramel continued eating her out. Jazmiine licked her nipples softly one by one. Carmen was pleased. Her vagina was getting licked lovely, and her nipples was a soft spot. "Haze, come put some dick in my mouth please," she called out. Haze laughed; he was more than ready to put his dick everywhere. Watching the girls touching and licking on each other had him almost ready to jerk off. He was glad it was his time. Carmen called for him to join in at the perfect moment. He got up from the bed where they had Carmen spread out pleasing her and went to get the cuffs from the couch. It was the first time that Carmen was sucking his dick and he wanted it to be special. He handcuffed her hands together. "You not stopping daddy from fucking this throat tonight," he told her. Carmen was in heaven. She loved all the freaky shit that was going on. She tilted her head back and told him her throat was all his. He slid his dick in her mouth slowly at first. Carmen sucked on his cock like it was a rib dripping million-dollar sauce. The harder Caramel licked on Carmen's pussy the harder she sucked on Haze's dick. Caramel stopped licking and began blowing on her vagina. It felt great to Carmen. All she could do was moan. Caramel then took her fingers and started playing with Carmen's clit.

Carmen kept moaning and moved the bottom of her body around in circles. "You like the way I'm licking on your punanie?" Caramel asked her. Carmen answered "Yes," as best she could with a mouth full of dick. "Babe can I put my dick in you now?" Haze asked. Carmen moved her head up and down keeping his dick in her mouth while answering. He took his dick out and uncuffed her hands. He told her to turn around. Before Carmen listened to him, she told Jazmiine to come lay down in front of her. Jazmiine was the oldest in the room, but she still did what she was told. Carmen turned around like Haze said and got on her knees. Her ass was up in the air and her coochie was ready for some dick. Jazmiine laid down in front of her with her legs spread out, butt naked. Carmen's fantasy was really coming to life. Caramel went back to the pole and gave Haze something to watch while he was fucking Carmen from the back. She'd dance until it was her turn. Haze felt like he was in a porno. He watched Carmen lick on

Jazmiine's box. He watched Jazmiine's fine ass moan and rub on her own titties and then he watched Caramel's naked black body dance on the pole. Everywhere he looked turned him on and made his dick harder. The whole scenario turned him on. There was no way he was ever going to leave Carmen. He wanted to marry her right then and there. He continued to pound on her pussy until it was time to switch. The e-pill had his manhood at full attention and filled with power. Carmen screamed and moaned like the dick tonight from Haze was something special. Carmen lost count of how many times Haze made her cum, and she needed a break. Haze's dick wasn't getting tired at all. "Daddy, can I take a dick break?" she asked Haze seductively. "Why babe, is the dick too much?" he asked as he continued to pound on her. "Yes daddy, the dick is too much. I need a break." Carmen cried out. Haze ignored her and kept pounding. Carmen was moaning uncontrollably again. "Say please and I'll let your pussy take a break," he told her. "Pleaseee?" Carmen moaned out. Haze slowed down on the pounding. He was slow stroking her now, not really wanting to stop. Carmen's pussy was juicy, wet, and warm. He could fuck her all night. He stopped stroking and let her up off her knees. "Who you want me to fuck next?" Haze asked Carmen, acknowledging that she was still in charge. Carmen had to catch her breath. "I want you to fuck Caramel next cause I know you've been waiting for that," Carmen winked as she spoke to her man. Haze smiled at Carmen, and she smiled back. "I love you," he whispered to her, and he meant it. He loved everything about her. She was so real and raw. "C, bring that pussy over here," Haze called out to Caramel. Carmen took immediate note of the nick name. She wanted to tell him right then '*ain't no fucking nick names nigga,*' but she let him have his way. Caramel couldn't wait to dance her ass over to his dick, but Carmen stayed calm. She actually liked that a female wanted her man. It made her want him more. She watched as Haze told Caramel to lay down on her back. Carmen took another note of him fucking her missionary style. Again, she stayed calm. She knew what she signed up for when she agreed to this fuck fest. The difference with this fuck fest though was that Haze was actually her man. There were feelings involved...heavy feelings, she thought. Whenever she went to "Pretty's Box," she went alone and was single. She thought this was going to be easy because of all the pleasure but now she wasn't too sure. *Tonight, might be the first and last Fuck Fest Friday of February,* she thought. Carmen decided to improvise. Instead of fucking Jazmiine while Haze fucked Caramel, she joined them. She literally threw her leg over Caramel's face and sat her pussy on it. If Haze was going to be staring at anything it was going to be Carmen's ass, not Caramel's pretty face, she thought. Haze laughed in his head and let out a moan. Carmen had him open. She was standing her ground and he loved it. Haze's moans turned Carmen on, and she knew she was doing something right. She turned around on Caramel's face and was now facing him. She stuck her tongue out and he sucked it while he stroked on Caramel. Haze and Carmen locked eyes and they connected deeper. The notes she took in her head during the night didn't matter at the moment. She was sitting on the face of the woman she thought would be an issue. And her man was kissing her while she was doing it. He was loving it. He didn't care about seeing Caramel. After cuming in her mouth, Carmen got up off her face. Haze watched as Caramel licked her lips tasting Carmen. He knew she tasted good. "I've been waiting to fuck you for free," Haze confessed to Caramel before pulling out of her pussy and cumming all over her titties. Her pussy was great, but he was done with it. Now he wanted some of her mouth. He had watched the way she pleased Carmen with her tongue, and he wanted to feel it too. "Come suck on daddy Haze's dick," he told her. Caramel did as she was told. Carmen wanted to spice things up. She picked her strap up and asked Jazmiine if she could fuck her. Jazmiine told her only if it was in the ass. Carmen thought twice. For some reason she wanted to fuck her pussy, but she figured she could take her ass first. Jazmiine walked over to the couch, got on her knees, and bent over the top of the couch. It wasn't too high. Haze sat next to her on the couch as Caramel was down on her knees sucking him off. Haze rubbed on the instructor's vagina as she waited for Carmen. It became wetter and wetter the more he played with it. Carmen walked over with her strap on and it startled Haze at first. This was actually his first time seeing some shit like this in person. He wasn't too sure how to feel. Caramel's head was out of this world. The way she moved her tongue around while sucking was amazing. Between the e-pill, the fine bitches, and this great head he

overlooked Carmen with the strap on.
It was her world, and he was just in it.
She fucked Jazmiine like the strap
belonged to her for real. Everything
turned into a fog for Haze. There was
freaky shit on top of freaky shit
going on. They all took turns
pleasing each other and Carmen used
each one of the toys she had laid out.
One minute she had a strap on, the
next minute she had vibrators in her
mouth fucking and licking pussy at
the same time. It was freaky, wild,
and nasty. They fucked for hours.

Haze fucked all three of them all different types of ways. They licked on each other, came on each other, and pleased each other for hours. The high and the horny joined together and made the time remarkable. At the end of it all Carmen kissed Caramel and Jazmiine goodnight before they left. After they were gone, she smoked another blunt and smiled at Haze. They had a successful night. "So, you're finished?" Haze asked Carmen before popping another e-pill. He wanted to please Carmen and thank her for the moment of a lifetime.

"Anything for you Haze," she smiled as she took a pill with him. They were going to be fucking for the next two days for sure.

February flew by with two more fuck fest Fridays. Each one of them were nastier than the last.

MARCH

March arrived and they agreed on **"Mistress March"**. They were both allowed to step out with an old or make a new mistress. Carmen had an ex she couldn't stop seeing no matter what. If it wasn't for Mistress March, she was bound to cheat with him. She never could go more than four months without seeing him. There was like a soul tie between the two of them as far as she was concerned. Although she knew she needed to see him for her soul, her heart couldn't stop wondering who Haze was going to see. She had to push these thoughts out of her mind as quickly as they came. She was going to see her forever nigga and Haze was going to see whomever he was going to see. That was it and that was all. To spice Mistress March up a bit they had to really move like they were sneaking around on each other. Neither of them had any say regarding who the other was going to see or when they were going to see them, they didn't have to say a word. The first day of Mistress March, Carmen woke up first. She thought nothing of it as she showered and headed out the door. She didn't want to dwell on Haze going out or see him getting ready. It was still a hard pill for her to swallow, knowing that he was going to be sleeping with other people. She focused on seeing her forever love, Money. Money was the freakiest and most caring man Carmen had ever met. She had no doubts in her mind that were it not for her sex addiction, they would've had a family together. Carmen messed up big time with Money and he'd never trust her again, but he would always fuck her. Carmen loved him and no one knew her body as well as he did.

491

Haze was a close runner up, but she had to see Money for her soul's satisfaction. As she pulled up to the hotel Money told her to meet him at, she felt butterflies. She missed Money but she missed Haze more. This was actually her first time fucking another man since Haze. There was a part of her that felt guilty, but she knew that Haze was going to be busy sleeping with his own person if he wasn't already. She needed to let go of her connection with Money anyway. She thought maybe she would make

Mistress March the last time she would sleep with him. She was going to get the dick for the rest of the month, and it would be the last time in her life, so she thought. When she got to the hotel room door the key was under the rug like Money had promised. He was laid out on the bed naked when she entered. She would usually jump right on him but this time she was hesitant. Haze was the last dick she had seen in person. She couldn't get Haze off her mind and it bothered her. She knew she was going to Fuck Money regardless, so she just wanted Haze to stay out of her thoughts. "Why you acting like you don't miss Big Daddy Money?" he asked, sensing the change in the way Carmen usually greeted him. "I'm sorry Big Daddy Money, I missed you so much," Carmen got herself together and forgot about Haze. She took her clothes off immediately and was ass naked. She walked over to Money and sat on the bed with him. "How much did you miss Big Daddy Money?" Money asked expecting

Carmen to prove it. Carmen knew what she had to do. She had to suck his dick and show him how much she missed him. When it came to Money, he was in charge. Carmen surrendered to him completely and did anything he told her to do. He was the only man who had her like that. "Let me find out you switching up on your big daddy," Money said, cautioning Carmen. "I would never," Carmen replied, knowing she could possibly be lying. This could be their last time together depending on how she felt afterwards. "I hope you wouldn't. I would hate to have to kill you," he replied. Carmen couldn't tell if he was joking or serious. He said it as if he was joking but also as if he meant it. Carmen loved Money but his response confused her. He made it clear that he couldn't trust her enough to be with her so she didn't understand why it would be a problem if they stopped fucking. Carmen thought about it for a second, she knew damn well that Money yearned for her the same way she fiend for him. She smiled, thinking about how she would probably kill his ass too if he tried to stop seeing her. Carmen felt stressed for a second and realized that she was too caught up in the moment. Yes, she loved Haze without a doubt, but Money was her first love, and he was part of the package. She was allowed to be doing what she was doing, and she wanted to enjoy it. She locked eyes with Money while she started licking his dick up and down. And that was all she needed to snap back into it. Before she was anybody's bitch, she was Money's. He taught her all she knew, and he turned her out. What she shared with Money was special to her. She told herself that it was the last time, but she knew that each time they slept together they bonded deeper. Carmen swallowed Moneys entire cock and balls like her life depended on it. She sucked him off for an hour easily. The sexual chemistry between them was out of this world. After making love to Money all over the room for hours, she was on her way back home. She looked just as good as she did when she'd left the house, so she didn't look like she was just getting down and dirty with another man. She wasn't sure if Haze was going to be home yet, but she picked up some takeout. She wanted to get home, shower, eat and lay down. Money had put the love making on her great today, like he had a point to prove. He was really letting Carmen know that she wasn't going anywhere. When Carmen got home, her place was a mess. You could definitely tell that Haze was home all day, just laying around being lazy. Dishes were piled up and there was junk food everywhere. She looked around and saw him fast asleep in the bed. Carmen felt stupid. Did her man really sit home all day while she was out cheating? She felt horrible. She felt like she had played herself. It was the beginning of Mistress March, and she couldn't wait to creep off. She didn't even think to sit back and see what Haze was going to do first. She made it obvious that she couldn't wait to get some new dick. Carmen was deep in her thoughts. She had to fix the situation she felt like she had ruined. She had to somehow get Haze to believe that she was out doing something else, anything other than cheating. She decided not to wake him, and she put the takeout in the microwave. She cleaned her entire home and made it like new without waking him. She took a nice long' hot shower and replayed her day with Money in her head. He wanted to see her again tomorrow, but Carmen couldn't get over the fact that Haze sat home all day. Carmen thought more on it and realized that even though Haze didn't go out today that didn't mean he was going to sit in the house for the rest of the month. He could have something set for any one of these days for all Carmen knew. She stopped beating herself up over stepping out on him. She would never know if he had something planned before she did her thang. And he had no proof that she was even doing her thang. They made this game and the rules for a reason. Carmen was not going to shame herself for living her truth. After her shower she put on some pajamas and went to bed. Her phone went off and it was a text from Money. He was telling her same time and place tomorrow. Carmen replied with, "ok," unsure of whether she was going to go.

The next morning Carmen overslept. She couldn't believe she slept in till noon. She was well rested thanks to Money. She rolled over and realized that Haze was out of bed. She got up to use the bathroom and looked for him all over. He was gone. Carmen took a deep breath before she panicked. She couldn't help but to think that this was Haze's time to step out on her. She just knew that after she went out all day, he was definitely going to do it back to her. She pushed Haze out of her mind and grabbed her phone to text Money. He was waiting for her. She had three missed calls from him when she checked her phone. She needed to hurry up. She called him back. "I'm sorry big daddy I overslept," she told him when he answered. "I'm on my way," Carmen threw some pants on and thought about Haze leaving again. The only way she was going to get her mind off him was by seeing Money. Part two today was going to be even better than yesterday. She grabbed a bag and packed a towel, wash cloth, a lingerie set, and a change of clothes. She was going to make the most of her time with Money while Haze was out doing him. This time she was spending the night, she wasn't coming home. She thought about

Haze one last time and shook her head before she left her home.

Haze ordered another drink from the bar. He had been sitting in the same spot since 8:00 AM drinking. He couldn't stomach the thought of Carmen being with another man. She had been out all day yesterday, came in the house, took a shower and slept like a baby. There was no way anyone could convince him that she wasn't out cheating. He hated that he couldn't even call it cheating because they agreed to this. Mistress March was stressing Haze the fuck out. He thought Carmen was gonna remix the game and sit her ass home or something, but she was the first one out the door. Haze had to understand it but he didn't want to. He was drinking his anger away and didn't think about cheating. After a few more drinks he decided to take his ass home. He hoped like hell that Carmen was there because if she wasn't, he was definitely going to step out on her.

"Carmen you better be the fuck in this house,", he called out when he reached home. No one answered. He started laughing as he looked at the time. It was 12:00 midnight and she wasn't home. "This bitch is fucking bold," Haze screamed out loud as he continued to laugh. He couldn't believe the way Carmen was giving it up. She was doing her thing two days in a row and the second day was even later than the first. Haze was pissed like a motherfucker. He wasn't sure how much longer he was going to be able to play this game. It sounded good when they agreed to do it but now it was getting the best of him. He knew there was a possibility that she could've been out with a girlfriend, but he had no idea in all actuality. "Aight Carmen, I looked at you differently but now I see you really ain't shit. Let's play then," Haze spoke out loud as if Carmen could hear him. He got on his phone and called up his favorite ex. "Yo Stacey, where you at?" Haze hadn't spoken to Stacey in a few months, but he knew that whenever he called her, she came. That's just how they were. There was never a time when Stacey didn't want dick from him. "Wow, now niggas know me. Let me guess, you miss this fucking tight grip, water park pussy, and these elite spits don't you boy?" Stacey asked confidently. She knew what time it was with Haze. He only called her when he wanted to fuck, and she didn't mind. She had her own thing going on. Haze was always a good big dick to fuck. "You know I miss that fucking water park, stop playing with me. Come see me right now. I got some liquor dick for you," Haze ordered. "Aight, drop ya location." Stacey had no problem coming to see him. Haze hung up and thought about what he was about to do. It was close to 1:00 AM now and he was certain that Carmen was going to stay out all night. If she didn't, she was going to wish that she did. Haze loved her but she wasted no time stepping out on him, so he wanted to beat her at her own game. He was thinking with intoxicated emotions. About 45 minutes passed and Haze's phone rang. It was Stacey letting him know that she was outside. Haze stumbled but made it to the door to let her in. He was trying his hardest not to fall over. "Boy you're too damn drunk to fuck. I know you ain't call me all the way over here to waste my time." Stacey was a little annoyed. Haze could usually control himself when he was drunk but now, he was looking sloppy. "And who the fuck house you got me up in trying to fuck? You real crazy. If you wanna fuck, you're coming with me. I'm out." Stacey meant her words. She didn't feel comfortable, and Haze was not fully alert. She was leaving with or without him. "Whatever then, go ahead and leave," Haze yelled. His head was spinning, and he was tired anyway. He wanted to fuck Stacey, but she took too long to come. He watched her leave as he laid on the couch. He was sleeping in the house alone and he had the worse thoughts of where Carmen was. Fucking Stacey would have taken his mind off of Carmen. He was upset at himself for getting so drunk. He thought about trying to get up and chase after Stacey. If he couldn't fuck, he could at least layup with her instead of being home alone, missing Carmen. He called her phone to see if she had pulled off already. "I know you ain't skurt off on ya favorite dick nigga like that," Haze spoke. "Haze you got 17 seconds to make it to my car or I'm out," Stacey revved her engine to let him hear it. "I'm coming Stacey baby, chill out," Haze told her then hung up the phone. He jumped up and shook his head. He had to get it together and make it outside. He walked to the kitchen sink and threw some water on his face. He was ready to go. He checked his pockets making sure that he had his keys. He locked the door and headed to Stacey's car. He watched his surroundings as he walked to her car. He didn't see anyone outside and he sure didn't see Carmen. It was well over 2:00 AM now. He felt no guilty conscience for leaving with Stacey. In his heart, he felt that Carmen had started it. She was supposed to sit this month out or at least let him lead. Haze felt a little soft being in his feelings, but it was just his thoughts getting to him. He was able to control his emotions and being with Stacey was going to make it easier. They rode off together and Stacey drove like a maniac. Haze sat back and enjoyed the air that came with her speeding. It woke him up and refreshed him, it was just what he needed. When they reached Stacey's house, he was more alert and could handle himself. He was ready to slide up in some warm pussy and fall asleep afterwards. He wasted no time taking his clothes off once he entered Stacey's room. He jumped in her bed and told her "Let's go," while beating on the bed. Stacey laughed at Haze; he was always funny to her. She would never say she loved Haze, but she definitely fucked with him more than any of her men. They had a dope bond. She took her clothes off and jumped in the bed next to him. She laid on her side and pushed her ass up on him. He kissed her neck and pushed his dick back against her ass.

He slid her panties to the side and shoved his long cock all the way inside her. Stacey let out a gasp and a moan all in one. Haze didn't take it easy. He was rough but he knew she loved it that way. Stacey liked to act like it was too rough for her but deep down inside she wanted him to go harder. Haze knew it, he would make her beg for him to go harder until she said couldn't take it. Then, he would keep going harder until he came while she screamed. That's the way he fucked Stacey. He pulled out and let his kids loose, all on her back and ass. She wiped them both off with a towel when he was finished and then laid back down. Haze wrapped his arm around her and cuddled with her. Stacey hated it and loved it at the same time. She loved it because she could get used to it, but that was also why she hated it. Because she could get used to it. Their relationship could never be serious, although Stacey would often wonder what it would be like. She drifted off to sleep and enjoyed the time she had with Haze. It was always short.

Carmen woke up at 11:00 AM the next morning and had to request a late check out. She was not ready to get up just yet. She and Money had made nasty sweet love all night and all morning. She took his penis like it was the last drop of it. She came to the decision that she wasn't going to see Money anymore. This was honestly going to be their last time. It was amazing but it still wasn't able to take her mind off of Haze. Money asked what was going on with her at least three times during their time together. Each time Carmen brushed it off like it was nothing, knowing that it was Haze on her mind. She would force herself out of her head and back into the groove with Money. Money felt it, but she cleaned it up so well that he overlooked it. He was gone when she woke up, but he made sure to leave her with a great goodbye before she went to sleep. Carmen laid down for another hour before she got up, showered, and headed home. She had no story at all for Haze, she was simply following the rules of Mistress March. Carmen came home to an empty house. It seemed as if Haze had stayed out all night or left early that morning, but she would never know. She was home now, and he wasn't. Carmen cared, but at the same time she didn't. She felt relieved knowing that she wasn't going to see Money anymore. She was going to stay home for the rest of March. She laid down in her bed smiling and feeling proud. She was finally going to leave

Money alone and he was always, always one of the reasons why her relationships didn't work out. She couldn't stay faithful. Besides her sex addiction, she had to have some of Big Daddy Money in her life. She had finally found someone who could make her leave him alone. Haze, and even though it broke her heart to step out on him, she had to do it to save their relationship for the long run. This sex game as their relationship was changing her for the better. She thought.

Carmen stayed home for the next three days, and Haze stayed gone. She cried every night that he didn't come home but she refused to call him. The game was the game. Three days turned into two weeks, and she was just about ready to call the whole game off. She didn't want to give up, but she couldn't take it anymore. She was doing the best she could trying to keep her mind off Haze, but she needed help. She picked her phone up to call Money. She was giving in and running back to him. Haze was hurting her feelings too much and she needed to ease them. She knew that Money would be able to fuck her mind right off Haze. She knew she was going to regret going back afterwards but she wasn't sure what else to do. She texted Money and told him she missed him. He replied by telling her to prove it. She knew what that meant. She packed her bag with more stuff than usual. She planned on staying the rest of March with him. There was only about a week and a half left. After packing, she turned off all the lights and TVs in her house. When she opened the door to head out Haze was standing there with his keys out. They both looked at each other and locked eyes. Carmen wanted to jump on him and hug him, but she was standing her ground. Haze wanted to choke her out, but he was staying calm. They stared at each other for a few more seconds until Carmen made the first move. She continued to walk out the door without saying anything. She continued to play the game and took this moment as a

chance to flip the switch on Haze.
Before she could get fully out the door
Haze questioned her. "Where the fuck
are you going Carmen?" Haze asked,
giving in. He didn't care. "Where the
fuck have you been Haze?" Carmen
asked since he started with a
question. "Bring yo ass in this house
Carmen, I'm not playing with you,"
Haze spoke seriously, and he was
stern. Carmen turned around and
walked her ass back into the house. It
turned her on a little bit that he
wasn't letting her leave. "I'm not

asking no questions except...are you done with Mistress March?" Haze asked Carmen. That was all he wanted and needed to hear. "I'm done," Carmen confessed. Haze grabbed her by her neck and play choked her. "You were gonna make me hurt your little ass," Haze joked, but was serious. He hugged Carmen and walked her further into the house. He grabbed her bagged and emptied it out all over the living room floor. He saw that she had lingerie in the bag and shook his head. He grabbed it and told her to put it on for him right then. They stayed in together for the rest of the month. No more mistress.

APRIL

April was now upon them, and they were both skeptical. The game had not been a walk in the park. They both decided on one of the best ideas for April. April was going to be "**Abstinence April Air**". April would be based on taking a breather and refraining from sexual activities.

During April they would take time to themselves to take in some fresh air and get in tune with themselves. They would make sure they were happy with themselves and that there were no distractions. They would focus on what they wanted for themselves and make sure that they were still working towards it. April would be all about thinking with a clear mind. Fresh air was always needed, and they would make sure they got it. April consisted of them going to the beach early mornings and breathing in fresh air. They appreciated life more, realizing how precious the air was. The air of the April mornings was working well for them. Their new morning routine made their days clearer. They missed their sex life, but the intimacy of just breathing fresh air and relaxing together was another level of bonding. They both loved it and didn't realize how much they needed it. They started meditating together in the fresh April air. This month relaxed them and cleared their minds. It was one of their best months yet. It was truly a breath of fresh air. Carmen was so proud of herself. She was able to go 30 days with no sexual activity. She was so pleased she made this game; the challenges were truly helping her addiction.

May

April influenced them to decide what May would be like. Together they agreed May would be "Manifestation Masturbation May". Carmen loved to masturbate; it was actually one of her favorite things to do. As always, Carmen wanted to spice it up. She didn't want to just masturbate the regular way. Before she met Haze she was working on her spiritual journey. One of the things she was interested in was the masturbation manifestation. She had tried it only once, but she was curious to know if it really worked. She thought it would be a great thing for them to do together. Haze only understood the masturbation part. He wanted to watch Carmen play with herself as he jerked off too. Carmen explained it to him." When you're jerking off what do you think about?" she asked him. "Be honest," she added in. "I mean, I watch porn, or I'll think about naked females," Haze laughed. "Ok so for Manifestation Masturbation May, you'll be changing your thoughts when you jerk off. Believe it or not masturbation is very important and the energy we give off while doing so is very strong. This month when you jerk off, fill your mind with all the things you want in your life," Carmen explained.

Haze thought about what she said. He had never really heard of or done any shit like this. Carmen noticed that he was thinking too hard about it. "Haze, it's the same as when you normally jerk off. But instead of naked women, let your personal goals and dreams fill up your mind. Really get in tune with seeing yourself living the life that you want. When you finish, you'll be releasing all of that energy into the universe. But you've got to believe it to manifest. The masturbation is just adding some razzle dazzle to help it come true," Carmen laughed. She tried to convince him the best way she knew how. "Ok, ok babe let's do it. Ima need your help though," he joked. Carmen was happy. Her relationship with Haze held the most experience. She was happy to know that he was willing to try new things with her. They would do their manifestation masturbation every Monday, Wednesday, Friday, and Saturday.

Their first time trying it Haze could not get it right at all. Carmen laughed at him the entire time. He was too tense and thought too hard about it. He couldn't get himself to cum. Carmen had to talk him through it with her bedroom voice. She made him close his eyes and take a few breaths to relax. When he was fully relaxed, she guided him with her words. "I want you to softly touch your manhood until he stands up on his own," Carmen whispered as Haze listened. "Now, I want you to think about where you see yourself in five years. Think about where you would

537

like to be and what you would like to have," Carmen paused and gave him a minute to think. She watched Haze smile and she figured it was working. "Think about how much money you'd like to have. Think about what you want your family life to be like. Think about the success you will achieve. Think about the good life that we all want to live deep down inside," Carmen spoke slow and soft. She noticed Haze's facial expressions seemed like he was concentrating. He was rubbing his penis harder and harder and even starting to moan. Carmen kept going. "Think about how healthy you will be physically and mentally. Think about the peace that will come with this life. Think about the feeling of finally having all your dreams come true," Carmen whispered. Before she knew it, Haze was letting out a loud moan and cum was flying everywhere. Carmen was so proud she licked some of his cum off his dick. "Good job bae," she acknowledged. Haze wanted to cry but in a manly way. Carmen was mind blowing and he was glad that he had found her. He kissed her with some of his cum still on her lips.

When it was Carmen's turn, she had no problems. She was a pro. She allowed Haze to sit back and watch her, but she didn't need him to speak. She laid across the bed and spread her legs open. She took a few deep breaths to relax herself, the same way she had told Haze to do when it was his turn. After relaxing, she closed her eyes and began touching all over her body. She rubbed her face her neck, her arms, and her thighs. She rubbed her stomach and the inside of her thighs. She gently rubbed over her vagina and went up to her breasts. She took her time rubbing her breasts and playing with her nipples. She started thinking about money. Not her ex but actual money. Since they were going to be doing this all week the whole month, she wanted to manifest masturbate one thing at a time. She pictured herself laying across a bed full of money. She pictured herself dancing around her room and throwing money everywhere around her. She pictured herself opening her closet and money just falling out. Money was turning her on. She was deep in her thoughts about money. She pictured herself jumping back on her large bed filled with money and the money just falling all over her. Carmen became too deep in her thoughts. She started picturing the money coming in between her legs, and before she knew it, she was fucking the money. Carmen was turned on and her fingers were rubbing her pussy like a DJ spinning a record. Haze sat back watching in amazement. Carmen was in another world, pleasing herself. It wasn't hard for Haze to know what she was thinking about because she started yelling out "money...yes money." He just watched. Carmen continued to think of the money actually fucking her until she came. She screamed out a satisfied scream and her body even started shaking. Haze was a little jealous, he couldn't remember ever making her cum so hard. He brushed it off and blamed it on the "manifestation masturbation". It had to be powerful like Carmen said. Carmen opened her eyes smiling and breathing deep. For a second, she forgot that Haze was there. She felt *amazing*. There was no doubt in her mind that she was going to be rich after this month was over. Her manifestation masturbation was just getting started.   Three weeks into Manifestation Masturbation May, Haze was feeling and walking different. He didn't need Carmen to guide him anymore and he had it down pat. He was manifestation masturbating more than three times on their assigned days now. He was open and all into it. He was so grateful for Carmen. She changed him without even knowing it. The beginning of the year was rocky with the games and even though April and May were beautiful, he knew that they still had many months to go. It was only a matter of time before Carmen would get back on her freaky shit and they would be wilding again. Haze wasn't sure what the next few months were going to bring but he was very sure of what he was going to agree with and not agree with. It had been Carmen's way since they'd been together, and he needed her to let go of being the boss. He didn't necessarily want to control everything, but when it came to their sexual life, he was going to take charge. Carmen was his now. He loved her and he wanted her. He wasn't into sharing what was his and he had no plans of Carmen leaving him anytime soon. Things were going to have to change.

JUNE

Manifestation Masturbation May finished and life was great...literally great. Dreams they masturbated to were coming to life, doors were opening to lead them to those dreams, and it was beautiful. They were both on top of the clouds. It was June now and they were at the half year mark.

They agreed that June would be "**Just let it out June**". If they had any secrets or wanted to get anything off their chests, they would just let it out. The other person had to agree to not get upset and each of them needed to be able to handle the truth. They would let their secrets out the first week of June and use the rest of the month to work on whatever the problems would be...if there were any. Carmen was a little nervous of what Haze was going to say but she had her confession all ready. Just let it out June was either going to make them or break them, but they both seemed ready for whatever.

"Okay babe so remember; we can get upset but we have to be able to handle the truth and accept whatever it is. You go first," Carmen instructed. Haze took a deep breath. "Okay Carmen," Haze paused. "Nah don't hesitate just let it out remember," Carmen reminded him. She was ready to hear whatever it was. "Carmen, I'm not really a sex addict. I lied. I was at the meeting that night

549

trying to find a new freak. I love all this shit you're into but it's becoming too much for me. I don't have the same sexual problems and strengths as you," Haze just let it out. It was too late for him to take it back, but he felt pretty good just letting it out. There was a long pause and Carmen just looked at him. Haze couldn't really tell if she was upset or not, but he waited for her to respond.

"Wow!" Carmen started. "I mean, I don't know how I should take that. First of all, babe, thank you for being honest and for going first. I feel like you are an undercover sex addict and you're in denial. I only say that because, why the fuck would you be going to sex addiction meetings to find girls like me? That's some different type of freaky shit. Or maybe you just thought there would be others like you out there doing the same thing? I mean, I guess...but speaking for the real ones out there, I was never faking this shit. This is a real addiction for me. I opened up and told you what made me this way and

you acted as if you understood.
That's cool though. Just as much as I
did this for us, I did this for myself.
And honestly, my secret feelings were
that I didn't wanna do this shit any
more. I was ready to change for you.
Now I know that you didn't go
through the same emotional changes
as me. I don't wanna do any of this
freaky shit anymore. I don't wanna
share you, I don't want nobody
touching you but mother fucking
Carmen. I know I would have to abide
by the same rules for you and I'm

ready. I fought off my demons these last few months because of you. I didn't want you doing any of that shit that we did but I had to get it out of my system. After Mistress March I was in my feelings big time. I felt like we were really cheating on each other and I hated it. All this time I thought you were fighting your own demons off too. This must have just been a freak show for you. See, it's lying ass men like you out there that make it hard for us women to trust. Why'd you act like a sex addict you fucking creep?" Carmen playfully punched Haze. Her 'just let it' out turned into a speech. She wasn't really mad at him, but she did feel a little played. She let his ass do all those things thinking that he really needed to do them. But at the same time, Carmen really needed them. She still helped herself due to his lie. It made sense to her in her own way.

"Let me express myself a little more so you can understand what I meant. I blurted it out quick because it was "just let it out June". So, I apologize if you took it the wrong way. What I meant was, I fucked up acting like I had a sex addiction. But I had no fucking idea that was gonna happen at the meeting. Carmen, you had me at my entrance. I saw you watching me because I was watching you, and the fact that you wanted me just as bad had me in awe. Everything about you makes my dick hard and my heart warm. I don't wanna play when it comes to you. I wanted to choke yo ass out during Mistress March when yo ass disappeared. I started second-guessing the rest of the months, I wasn't sure how much more I could take. Don't get me wrong, I can get jiggy with the ladies but the thought of another man touching you killed me. I love you. And I've never been with a sex addict before, you really taught me a lot. I'm sorry I lied but I'm happy you got that shit out of your system. You're beautiful Carmen, and you don't have to share your body to feel that way anymore. I'm here for you, I'm here for it all. I'll do whatever you need me to do to you sexually, but sharing you isn't an option anymore. So, if you're really ready to change, I'm here for it, but if you wanna finish the year out on this shit, I'm tapping out. So, it's on you what's it gonna be?" Haze finished his speech leaving Carmen teary eyed. She loved this vulnerable side of him. She couldn't believe a made-up sex game had taught them both so much. Carmen loved Haze without a doubt, but he was sneaky. She was willing to work with it though. She looked forward to the next six months with just them. She would for sure find out if she was changed or not.

To Be Continued...

Penelope

I scheduled reservations for dinner tonight babe, so you don't have to cook, Renee smiled as she read her text from her soulmate. Oh really, may I ask where? she texted back right away waiting for a response. Does it matter? You know I know all your favorite places. Just dress up pretty the way I like you to. He texted back. Renee was blushing, she was head over hills in love with this guy. His name was Omar Crews, and he was beautiful. Renee felt like he was sent from heaven. After the unbearable heartbreak she went through with her ex, Onyx Dane, she knew she deserved this. Onyx was her daughter's father and her first love, but things between them were horrible. As much as she hated him though, she never interfered with him and their daughter's relationship. So, regardless of what she couldn't get away from him. Onyx was once the love of Renee's life. Back in the days of them being together, you couldn't tell her nothing about her man. She was 18, a virgin and fresh out of high school when they met. Now, Onyx was older, seven years older to be exact. He was fine as hell, in the streets heavy and had made a big name for himself. From the moment they saw each other, they both just knew they were going to last a lifetime.

Renee was in the library studying for an entrance exam the first time she saw Onyx. He walked through like a man with honor. As sad as it sounds, she had never seen such a fine black man in her library before. There were mostly nerds and younger boys playing around on the computers. She wondered what the hell he was doing there. Onyx walked past the table she was sitting at and they both locked eyes. Renee couldn't help but to smile at him, she had no control over her facial expressions. Onyx just looked, and kept it moving...no smile, no smirk. Renee felt a little embarrassed. She knew that she was pretty as hell so she couldn't understand why he just brushed her off. She rolled her eyes and went back to studying.

After about an hour more of studying, she was ready to go. When she walked out to her car, she noticed an orange rose laying across her windshield which immediately caused her to look around. She saw no one around and picked up the rose. Under it was a handwritten note in the most beautiful handwriting she had ever seen. She wondered if someone really wrote it or had it printed. The note read; I saw you looking, sure hope you ain't tooken. 347-458-0610 holla at me. - Onyx. Renee busted out laughing. She laughed so hard that she had to take another look around to make sure no one was watching her. She put the note in her pocket and drove off, thinking hard about this mystery man. She had no idea how he knew her car or why he wrote a note instead of saying something himself. But one thing she did know was that she was going to call him as soon as she reached home. Onyx was getting his balls licked when his phone started ringing. He looked at the caller id and didn't recognize the number. He looked down at Nita sucking his dick and didn't want to make her stop. But if this was business calling, he had to be fully alert and that was almost impossible whenever Nita the eater was sucking him off. Nita the eater was a nick name he had given her because her head game was immaculate. Nita sensed that he was thinking about answering his phone, so she started giving him more of a reason not to. He put his phone down laid his head back and enjoyed his time with her. He knew with females that's all it ever was, your turn for the moment.

He never got attached, and he never gave a woman the chance to break his heart. Being raised by his father, who in his eyes was a sucker for love, he had seen all the scandalous things women could and would do. If you let them. After Nita finished wiping her mouth off, Onyx got up to grab a towel. He didn't have to say much. Nita already knew the routine. She fixed herself, said "see you later" and headed out the door. Onyx didn't look back, he headed to the shower to clean himself off. He never let a female stay over after they finished their business no matter how good it was or how late it was. He wasn't rude but he was a man of his word and he meant it when he said, "after I hit, you gotta dip." After a nice shower his phone rang again. It was the same unknown number from earlier. This time he answered. "Yo," he said as he answered his phone. "Umm hello," a soft voice he had never heard before responded. "Yo, who this?" He was a little confused until he thought about it. All his women's numbers were stored, this had to be the girl he saw in the library. Before he could fix his words, she responded "I guess you got so many girls calling you huh?" Renee spoke trying to flirt. "Nah, what's up Ms. Library. I know who this is," he responded throwing her off guard. Renee smiled on the other end of the phone. For some reason he gave her butterflies and she loved it. "Ms. library huh? My name is Renee actually. How'd you know what car I was in?" she was curious to hear this. "I know everything little lady but listen I'm tired Ima have to hit you back. And good luck on your entrance exam." He tried to end the conversation. Renee wasn't feeling how he was trying to brush her off yet again. "Well damn, nice talking to you too. And thank you, have a good sleep," Renee hung up without giving him a chance to say bye. Once again, she felt like she was too thirsty, and he was trying to play her. She wondered how the hell he knew about her test. For a second, she wondered if he was crazy. She didn't care though, he looked too good. Onyx looked at his end of the phone and felt some kind of way over how she just hung up. Before he knew it, he was calling her back and he usually never did that. "Yo," Renee said, answering her phone. Onyx smiled, for some reason he liked how she was sounding like him. "You have *a good sleep too," was all he said before he hung up. He looked at his phone again a little confused. That was the first of him letting a girl make him do something petty. He didn't like it already. He drifted off to sleep and thought about his next money move.*

Three days later, Renee was at the gas station getting

gas. As she pumped, she
realized that her back tire
was flat again. She was so
tired of her car, but she loved
it. It was all she had. It got
her from point A to point B
with very little problems. It
was a hand me down from
her older sister, so she
appreciated it. After getting
gas she pulled over to the air
machine. She went inside, got

quarters, and came out in a rush. She was already late for work and still had to get something to eat for lunch. "Do you need help with that?" Renee heard a familiar voice ask her and she realized that it was her current crush, Onyx. "Yes, I do, I think I need my tire changed and my radiator was over heating," Renee pouted as she lied. She

wanted to see how much he
was willing to help her and
how much of his time she
could get. She wasn't sure
what it was about him, but he
gave her the craziest
butterflies. She thought this
was fate, seeing him again,
and she didn't wanna let him
get away. Onyx looked at her
car and then looked at her.
He had fell for her pretty

face the moment he saw her in the library, but he was there to conduct business as usual so he couldn't get caught up. Now he had the time to truly admire her. Renee was beautiful. She was dark skinned with dimples and bright eyes. Her hair was naturally curly and long as hell. Now that he was looking at her good, he could tell that she was young. "How old are you?" he asked. "I'm 22," Renee lied again. "You busy right now?" he asked her. "Nope," Renee lied for the third time in less than five minutes. She knew that she was supposed to be at work an hour ago, but Onyx had her in a daze. "Park your car and come with me," Onyx demanded as he turned to walk back to his own car. That was all Renee needed to hear. She didn't think twice about it.

Renee had no idea where she was going but she was simply happy to be by this mystery man's side. About 15 minutes after getting into his car and pulling off, she heard sirens pulling them over and she became nervous. Onyx looked in his rearview and then looked at her. "Yo, I know this is our first date and all, but can you hold some shit for me? I got a license and shit, but you know how these pigs can be sometimes." Onyx tried to hand Renee a bag of what looked like coke. She was shocked. For a minute she thought about everything that occurred in the last half hour. She was missing work, left her car at a gas station to ride around with a stranger and now he wanted her to hold his drugs. For some reason, all Renee could hear was "I know this is our first date" and she just reached her hand out for him to pass her the drugs. She didn't say anything. She simply put the drugs in her panties. Onyx was baffled. He didn't know if this was a good or bad thing that she took the drugs so easily. He pulled over and waited for the cops to walk to his window. "License and registration please," the cop asked. Onyx handed him his information and the cop walked back to his car. He came back quickly, gave him his paperwork back and told him to have a nice day. Renee was sweating and was finally able to breathe easy. "So, where's our first date again?" she asked as she removed the drugs from her panties and handed them back to him. Onyx smiled. He opened his phone and texted his homeboys, "good job". He always had them playing as cops when he needed to test a new bitch out. Renee passed.

Omar was nothing like Onyx, he was calm cool and collective. He was everything Renee never knew she needed. The heartbreak that Onyx caused her was so bad that she thought she'd never be able to love again. But she was, and now Omar was her dream man. She thought about what she was going to wear to dinner. Omar loved when she dressed sexy, which made it extra fun picking out an outfit. For some reason she wanted to wear something new and fresh. She wanted to go shopping. She yelled out for her daughter Penelope to come to her. She smiled watching her beautiful baby girl walk in. "We're going out to dinner with Omar tonight so let's go shopping," Renee smiled. Penelope smirked back but said nothing. "Now don't you want a new baby doll?" Renee asked her. She would always have to bribe Penelope to shop with her. Sometimes Renee's hours of shopping would stress Penelope out. "Yes, and I know which one I want too"

Penelope replied excited about shopping now. Renee laughed. She prepared them both to head out.

Renee skimmed the racks as she tried to find the perfect dress. Penelope stood back and watched. "Mommy, I wish you were getting dressed up for daddy," Penelope confessed to her mom out of nowhere. Renee stopped moving the hangers and gave her undivided attention to her 6 ½ -year-old daughter. "Honey, what's the matter? I thought we talked about this. I thought you liked Omar?" Renee was shocked to be hearing this come up again. It took her a while to move on from Onyx, and she never pressured her daughter into accepting any other man in her life. Penelope hated the thought of her mom being with anyone other than her dad, but eventually she got over it. So, Renee thought. "I'm sorry mom, I know he makes you happy. Forget it," Penelope replied. "No, the hell I will not Penelope!" Renee held Penelope's cheeks and looked her in her eyes while speaking. "Now you listen to me. You are the most important person in my life. You come before anybody. So, if there's a problem, you just let your momma know. I wouldn't be with him babe if you didn't give the okay. Don't you ever forget that you hear me?" Renee spoke in a serious tone. "I know mommy, I'm sorry," Penelope hugged her mom. Renee felt awful. "Don't be sorry babe, you could tell me anything you feel." She tried her hardest to make her family work, but Onyx just kept fucking it up. She knew in the long run that their daughter would suffer the most, but she had to choose to honor her own peace of mind over all of them. Being with Onyx was only leading her toward a mental institution or jail. She saw no fairytale ending and knew she had to get out. Renee thought finding a good man was going to solve the problem, but it only eliminated the problem temporarily. It's true that there is nothing like your real father. She hugged Penelope back as she thought about canceling dinner with Omar.

The thought of her daughter being upset over her man didn't sit right with her. After leaving Onyx, it was just Renee and Penelope for two years. The bond they developed while living alone was amazing. Now, a year and some change in of dating and living with Omar, she knew that Penelope was still adjusting to the changes. She took a deep breath and continued to choose an outfit from the racks of clothes.

Omar smiled at the 2-carat engagement ring he was proposing to Renee with. He hoped like hell that she was ready and loved him as much as he loved her. Judging from their relationship, she had most definitely proved her love, but Omar always had a fear of losing her to Onyx. He knew about their terrible past, but he also knew about their deep bond. And the fact that they had a child together didn't make it any easier for him. He knew that once he proposed, things would have to change, and when she became his wife, the changes would become final. The first time Omar saw Renee, it was 6:25 AM on a Monday morning, and she was new to his job. She was an LPN at his hospital where he was a doctor. He noticed her beautiful new baby face among the crowd right away. She wore a white uniform with white sneakers and pink socks. He remembered this day like it was yesterday.

Her hair was in a ponytail with a long curl, and she wore diamond studs. He approached her and welcomed her to the team. "Welcome to Langston Hughes Hospital gorgeous" his direct compliment caused Renee to tense up a little. "It's Renee but thank you. I stand out that much as a newbie huh?" she asked jokingly.

"You're all I see on the floor," Omar was direct with his compliment again. Renee was indeed beautiful, and he hadn't seen real beauty in a while. She smiled and shook her head. "Well thank you, Dr. Crews, is it?" Renee read his name tag. "Very welcomed," he said, as he began to walk away. The way she said his name turned him on and he was afraid that if he stood there any longer, she'd be able to tell. He had to get to the bathroom and check himself, something like this hadn't happened since his school days. This woman had touched his soul. In the bathroom he splashed water on his face and gazed into the mirror. "Pull yourself together O, you're acting like you've never seen a beautiful woman before," he spoke to himself as he giggled. He walked out of the bathroom and decided that day that Renee would be his wife. And he would do anything to have it that way.

Almost two years later, here he was ready to get down on one knee. He had just a few more hours until dinner and he wanted everything to be perfect. Omar took his phone out of his pocket and dialed his party planner to make sure things were running smoothly. As promised, everything was on point. All he had to do was get ready and wait for his beautiful soon-to-be-wife to arrive. He decided to text her. "You don't have to drive, there will be a limo waiting." The three bubbles that shows when you're texting on an iPhone popped up quickly and bubbled for a few moments. He knew she was trying to figure out what to say. After a few more seconds of the bubbles popping up and stopping, a text saying "I love you" came through. Omar smiled and reacted to the message with a heart. He was about to see just how much she really loved him.

Back home, Renee couldn't wait to try on her new fits. She had almost an hour before the limo would be arriving and she knew how bad she was with time. But she wasn't sure which one she was going to wear. She tried the first dress on, and it fit her just right. It was a little black dress, but it was sexy, and it complimented her figure perfectly. It was low cut in the front and showed just enough cleavage. It stopped above her knees and showed her thick thighs off. It was cut out in the back showing her rose tattoo. She loved it but had more to try on. The next dress was super tight-fitting and hugged her hourglass shape flawlessly. It was all white and stopped a little under her knees. She looked like an angel in this dress, and she loved it. Without trying on anything else she made up her mind that this was her outfit for the occasion. She hadn't worn white in a while anyway. She

took the dress off and decided
to get Penelope ready first.
Giving her a quick bath, she
admired how beautiful her
daughter was. One thing
about Renee was that she
loved her child more than life
and she always became
emotional whenever she
thought about being a
mother. Her mind was still
on Penelope's comment

earlier about her father and it made her realize how much they'd been through. Onyx was the most toxic man she had ever been with and although she had a blast with him, she outgrew him and his way of seeing life. She tried to change him for years and it almost killed her. What hurt her the most was the fact that he was such a loving father and made himself look like a saint to Penelope. He would never ever show his true side around his daughter. It was as if he was a totally different person. It hurt Renee to know that he had the ability to love and do right for their daughter, but not for the both of them. Yes, Renee agreed, their daughter was the most important woman in his life, but she was the one who carried her into this world. She wanted the same love and respect, if not more. Penelope would never understand the damage Onyx has done and would have continued to do if Renee didn't leave. In Penelope's eyes, everyone wanted a daddy like hers. Renee loved how much she loved her

father, but it was bittersweet.
She oiled Penelope's body
down and began getting her
dressed, "Mommy, where are
we going to eat?" she asked in
her baby voice. "I don't know
beautiful, it's a surprise,"
Renee answered honestly.
Penelope didn't say anything
else. Renee dressed her in a
pretty pink dress with white
ruffled socks and pink shoes.

She looked just as stunning as her mother. "Okay babe, now sit still and stay pretty while mommy gets just like you," she smiled as she spoke to her daughter. Penelope had Renee and Onyx's face mixed perfectly together and was blessed with the green-eyed trait from her grandmother. Renee had about 30 minutes to get ready and she spent 20 in the shower. The limo would have to wait for her, like everyone else...like always. She oiled herself down quickly and put on a sexy black thong and matching bra. She slid her dress on and admired herself in the mirror for a second. It looked even better the second time on. She combed her wrap down and her hair complimented the dress. She finished it off with chunky stud earrings and the watch Omar had bought her a few months ago. She looked amazing and she knew it. The ringing of her phone interrupted her moment of amazement. It was Omar, and she knew he was wondering what was going on. She didn't answer. Instead, she let it go to voicemail and then checked her text messages. Like she assumed, he was letting her know that the limo was outside. She hurried and put her shoes on and grabbed jackets for her and Penelope. "Let's go P, the limo is here," she told her. "Mommy, we look too pretty tonight," Penelope's soft voice spoke and it warmed Renee's heart.

"Yes, we do baby...too damn pretty," Renee smiled at Penelope. She had a confident daughter and she loved it. Renee walked outside to a green stretch limo with the door opened waiting for her. A beautiful female driver stood waiting for her and Penelope. Renee smiled. For a second, she felt bad for having her waiting. They entered the limo and sat anxiously waiting to arrive at the restaurant. The drive was a little longer than expected. She wondered where these reservations were made. She texted Omar and asked him where the hell they were going. He responded and told her to just relax and enjoy the ride. She knew he was up to something now, but she had no idea what. After driving for a little over a half an hour, they finally came to a stop. She had never seen this restaurant before. "I thought he said it was one of my favorite places," Renee spoke to herself, looking out of the window. "Enjoy your night Miss," the driver told her. Another beautiful woman opened the limo door to greet Renee and Penelope. "You ladies must be the Long's, please follow me..." Renee was greeted by her last name and loved it. This lady had a Jamaican accent and was so polite. Renee was taking in every little detail. She wondered what today was and made sure that she didn't forget whether it was their anniversary of being together. Omar was being extra special tonight but at the same time, that's just how he was. He was spontaneous and always surprising her with sweet new ways to show her love.

She followed the lady into the restaurant, and it was beautiful. Absolutely beautiful. The chandeliers were sparkling and amazing. The table setting was like something she had never seen before. The Silverware was made of diamonds. The napkins were silk. The glasses sparkled with diamond trimming on the bottom. It was simply beautiful. She had never seen anything like it before. "Mommy, is this a place for only princesses to eat?" Penelope asked even more fascinated than her mom. "Yes baby, this is exactly where the princesses come to eat," Renee replied as she stood in awe until the beautiful escort asked her to keep following her. She took her to the back of the restaurant and through a door. She entered a room that was dimly lit but you could still see. It took a second for Renee's eyes to adjust to the light change. She became confused as to why the room looked like a hospital at first until it hit her. Renee's eyes watered as she looked around the room and took everything in. Omar made her feel like she was right back at the day they first met. She remembered exactly how she *was feeling. She was finally over Onyx completely. She wasn't crying at night anymore or missing him. She wasn't forgetting that he wasn't taking the garbage out on Tuesdays anymore. She wasn't afraid of living alone anymore. She didn't crave him at random times of the day anymore. She wasn't addicted anymore. She was* able to look at her daughter and not feel like she had failed her. She had accepted that she couldn't have a family with him like she dreamed of. She wasn't necessarily ready for a man, but she was ready to be back in the field. Her new job she prayed for had finally come through. She was doing well for herself and most of all,

Penelope was happy. It was her first day at work and here stood this fine ass chocolate doctor complementing her. A man hadn't made her smile in years. Her heart was skipping a different beat than when it skipped with Onyx. Her heart was fluttering, and she wasn't sure if it was a good thing, but it felt great.

She still held her composure while her insides went crazy.

Renee couldn't control her tears. She turned around and saw Omar on one knee and she became overwhelmed. She couldn't speak and ask him if he was dead ass serious right now. He held out a yellow ring box, knowing that yellow was her favorite color. "Renee, you're still all I see, will you marry me?" As soon as he finished his question the dimmed lights brightened up and Renee saw her family and close friends all around standing in uniforms making the day more real. Renee punched him in his chest before turning to run away. She stopped, turned back around, grabbed the ring then continued to run away to the bathroom. Omar just laughed as he stood up. "Excuse me y'all," he told the family before heading after his girl. Renee was in the mirror fanning herself to stop crying. Omar walked up to her and hugged her. Renee cried in his arms. "Why would you do that to me in front of everybody? Yo, I had no hints or nothing," Renee cried and laughed at the same time. "Omar, my heart is overjoyed right now baby. I love you so freaking much. This was beautiful. I feel exactly how I felt when you first spoke to me. I feel like I'm in a fairytale," Renee kissed her man deeply. After kissing for a minute Omar asked, "So is this a, yes?"

while laughing. "It's a, I'll suck your dick right now yes," she laughed. They kissed again. "Okay so can we go do that over please? The people need to be clear about what's going on," Omar laughed again. "Yes, yes go head go back," she told him while filled with humor.

"Okay guys, Renee doesn't do too well with surprises. We

gotta do it over," Omar told the family after coming out the bathroom. Everyone laughed knowing Renee and stood back in position. Renee walked out of the bathroom and admired the room again, feeling the same way when she first seen it. When she turned around again, she saw Omar behind her on one knee. She made a surprise face and put her hands over her mouth. "Renee Rose Long, you're still all I see. Will you marry me?" he asked her again like it was the first time. The dimmed lights became bright again. "Omar, I would marry you over and over and over again." Tears fell from her eyes as he slid the ring on her finger. He picked her up and kissed her deeply. Everyone filled the room with awes, and handclaps. They kissed like no one was around. A few moments later, Renee went to find Penelope in the crowd. "Hey beautiful," she hugged her daughter as she was ready to share the news with her. "Mommy, what's going on are we having a party and are you getting married mommy?" Penelope asked. She was already aware of what was going on, but she wanted her mother to explain it fully. Renee took Penelope to a quiet part of the restaurant. "Yes baby, mommy will be getting married. Omar asked me to be his wife so we're having a party to celebrate," Renee explained with joy in her heart. "So is daddy coming to the party too?" Penelope asked. "Yes, he's just running late," Renee smiled. She knew how much Penelope loved her father and he would always have to be a part of their life. And it was true, he was invited to the party, he was just running late.

Everyone enjoyed themselves and the party

went on for a few hours before it ended. Renee watched in bliss as her family came together to celebrate her happiness. Onyx and Omar were getting along well. Renee had no problem with Onyx bringing a date. He didn't have a girlfriend after Renee, but he had bitches. It was beautiful, and most of all she was going to be a wife.

Back at home now, she kept replaying the entire night in her head. She was overwhelmed with joy and love. She was feeling amazingly special. She was tucking Penelope into bed when she noticed a sad look on her face. "Now what's the matter with my beautiful baby?" Renee asked Penelope in a kiddish voice. Penelope didn't respond. This wasn't like her. "Baby what's wrong?" Renee asked more seriously now. Penelope said nothing and started crying. "Penelope, talk to your mom and tell me what's going on right now!" Renee was worried and wanted to know what was wrong. "Mommy I don't want you to marry Omar. Mommy, he does bad things to me," Penelope cried as she spoke. Renee's heart stopped. It was as if she was out of her mind, body and soul and she had to bring herself back. She wasn't sure she was hearing her six ½ - year-old baby girl correctly and she hoped like hell that she wasn't. "Baby what did you say?" she asked her in the softest voice. "Mommy, Omar does bad things to me. Please don't marry him," she cried harder as she repeated her words. Renee grabbed her daughter and held her tight. "Baby, mommy is right here. Nobody will ever hurt you again. Tell mommy what he did baby," Renee tried to fight her tears back, as she didn't want to scare Penelope, but her entire soul broke hearing her daughter's words. Hate for Omar filled her mind and body instantly. Penelope was quiet and kept crying. Renee held her daughter and couldn't hold back the tears anymore. They cried together. "Baby, I need you to tell mommy what he did to you," Renee asked her again. "He touches my pocketbook mommy," she told her mom. Her pocketbook was their codeword for her vagina. Renee was beyond furious. "Okay baby come on. I'm taking you to daddy's house," she told her as she got her up out of bed. She had heard enough. She calmed herself down as her mind continued racing. She didn't

want to alert Omar that
something was wrong. She
walked into their bedroom
and saw him fast asleep. She
shook him to wake him up.
She couldn't even say his
name, she felt disgusted.
"Penelope isn't feeling well,
I'm going to bring her to her
dads," Renee told him. Omar
thought it was awkward, but
he never questioned her

about her daughter. She made it clear to him from day one that wasn't his place. "Ok, hurry back babe," he spoke after rolling back over to sleep. Renee wanted to cut his tongue out his mouth and slit his throat right then and there. His voice no longer turned her on. His words disgusted her. She put Penelope in the car and told

her she would be right back.
She came back inside and
went to her secret safe. She
learned from Onyx to always
keep this. She took her gun
out and held it behind her
back. She walked back to her
bedroom and stood over
Omar while he slept. Tears
fell down her face as she
starred at him. He looked like
a sleeping angel. Her heart

was hurting so bad, and she was devastated. She couldn't understand how she let something like this happen to her daughter in her own home. She took the gun and hit him as hard as she could in his face. Omar jumped up out of his sleep screaming, "What the fuck?" He saw Renee standing over him pointing a gun at him. "Yo

Renee, what the fuck is wrong with you?" Omar yelled and cursed. Renee had never heard him speak this way, or in this tone. It made her feel like there was definitely a side of him she never knew existed. Renee pointed the gun at the man she just had the most love for in the world. The man she just said yes to...to being his wife. The man who showed her real love and allowed her to love again. The man she trusted around her daughter, and who she now learned had violated that trust in the worst way possible. Touching Penelope would be the last thing he remembered in his life. "How could you touch my fucking daughter, Omar?" she asked him disgusted.

"What the fuck? Renee what the fuck are you talking about?" Omar asked confused. "Bitch how the fuck could you disrespect me like that?" Omar replied with anger and base in his voice. Renee was appalled, he had never ever called her a bitch before...ever. Renee flipped. "I hope you rot in hell you sorry son of a bitch. How could you touch a baby? I'll show you a fucking bitch alright." Renee closed her eyes and pulled the trigger repeatedly. She couldn't stop. When she opened her eyes all she saw was Omar, bloody on the floor. Without thinking, she dropped the gun and ran out to her car. She wiped her face as best she could, not wanting to scare Penelope. She got in the car and looked Penelope in her eyes, "Omar will never be able to hurt you again baby." Renee turned around and sped off, unclear of what was really going on. She had just murdered the love of her life, but she would do it again for her daughter. She was numb. The thoughts in her mind of her daughter being touched ate at her soul. The *thoughts of her daughter being abused and wondering where her mom was, ate at her soul. The thoughts of her daughter crying while being taken advantage of by a nasty grown man ate at her soul. Her mind was gone. She drove to Onyx's house hoping he would be able to understand and not hate her for letting this happen.*

Pulling up at Onyx's house, she couldn't control her emotions. She didn't care about Penelope seeing her hurt anymore. She was hurting over her anyways. Renee grabbed her and got out of the car. She banged on Onyx's door until he answered. "Who the fuck is that banging on my door?" he came screaming. "It's Renee,

Onyx. Open the door!" she cried. Hearing Renee's voice startled him. He opened the door and she fell into his arms. "What the fuck is going on Renee? Penelope, baby what's going on?" Onyx changed his voice when he started speaking to her. "I killed Omar," Renee cried. "What you mean Nae? what happened?" Onyx was shocked. He knew Renee well enough to know that she was telling the truth. The state she was in told it all. "He was touching on Penelope. I had to do it," Renee said in a low voice. Onyx threw Renee off him. "What the fuck you mean he was touching on my daughter?" Onyx was ready to kill her and go make sure Omar was indeed dead. He grabbed Renee by her neck and started choking her. "How the fuck was that motherfucking scum bag able to do that?" he screamed as he squeezed her neck harder. Renee tried to fight but he was too strong. Penelope was screaming and jumping up and down. "Daddy, stop! Stop hurting mommy daddy, I lied. I lied. Omar never touched me. I'm sorry. I just want you and mommy to be together daddy please stop." Penelope yelled out, and Omar released Renee. "I'm so sorry for lying mommy. I just want you to marry daddy. I lied! Omar didn't hurt me. I pinky promise he didn't hurt me mommy." Penelope's soft voice screamed. Renee looked at her and felt numb. Reality

started to sink in. Her
daughter lied and she killed
her other half. She asked no
questions when it came to
Penelope. And it turns out
she had lied. She lied over her
father who was a toxic son of
a bitch. "You son of a bitch,
this is your fucking fault!"
Renee charged at Onyx, and
he just grabbed her and held
her tight. He couldn't

imagine how she must have been feeling and he realized that he was wrong for choking her. If it were true, it wasn't her fault. She had to find a man. It's his, for not changing for his family. He allowed another man to be able to get that close to his daughter. Penelope's lie made Onyx realize what was truly important in life. The family that he had created. He felt like a scumbag himself for all the shit he had done to Renee in the past. He knew that she didn't deserve it, but he never knew real love. His mom never showed him any. As he held Renee, he grabbed Penelope and hugged her too. A few seconds about 6 cop cars pulled up with flashing lights and screams to freeze.

Onyx knew they were there for Renee. He wished he could save her, but he couldn't. There was no time. "Where's the gun?" he asked her. "I left it," Renee began to cry like a baby. No fucking way did she want to go to jail for murder. "Renee Long, you are under arrest for the questioning in the attempted murder of Omar Crews." Renee's heart pounded. Attempted murder...she thought. That meant Omar was still alive. She cried like a baby as they cuffed her, and Penelope screamed. "No mommy I lied! I said I lied! Why are they taking you?" Penelope didn't understand the damage that her lie had caused. She didn't know what was going on. Renee cried harder as she watched Onyx pick Penelope up and bring her tiny screaming body in the house. "I'm coming for you, don't say nothing. Not a fucking word" was the last thing she heard from Onyx before she was hauled off in a police car.

To Be Continued...

!! NOTE FROM THE AUTHOR !!

If you made it here **THANK YOU!** I hope you enjoyed my quick little stories. I'd like to hear some feedback from you guys! Leave a review on any of my pages please. I want to know which story should make it to Quickie part 2? Who was your favorite character? What story did you enjoy the most? When do you want me to drop the next parts? Where in the book had you the most **FUCKED UP**? Why would I only have five stories? Should I add more next time? (I'm thinking 7 to spell out Quickie) What was bad about them? What was the best thing? I want to hear it all! lol. If you don't already, go follow my pages. Instagram @prettylittlewriter_ Facebook @ Author AC Irving, twitter @prettywriterAC. AND THANK YOU ALL again! — A.C